Louie's Snowstorm

Louie's Snowstorm

E. W. Hildick

Illustrated by
Iris Schweitzer

Doubleday & Company, Inc.
Garden City, New York

Library of Congress Cataloging in Publication Data

Hildick, Edmund Wallace.
    Louie's snowstorm.

    SUMMARY: Louie tries to beat a Christmas snowstorm and give his
customers the usual good service despite the girl "observer" aboard his
dairy truck.
    [1. England—Fiction]   I. Schweitzer, Iris, illus.   II. Title.
PZ7.H5463Lr   [Fic]
ISBN 0-385-06452-7 Trade
ISBN 0-385-00025-1 Prebound
Library of Congress Catalog Card Number 73–20822

Contents

Contents

Louie's Snowstorm

Chapter
One

The
Christmas
Spirit

There was trouble in the air.

It was reflected in the eyes of Louie Lay as he drove back to the dairy that morning. Gray eyes, with ominous glints. Gray as the sky over the sprawling English town. Gray as some of the streets they were rattling through. Louie's eyes seemed to be absorbing it all. All that grayness. All that trouble. Soaking it all in. Concentrating it all into those two narrow slits. Putting a polish on it there, giving it a menacing glitter—ready to shoot it right back at the first likely target.

The two boys sitting up front with him didn't notice it.

Normally, Louie's helpers were the first to read such signs. Tim Shaw had reached the stage where he didn't even have to see the milkman's eyes. Little things like the tightening of the skin on the smooth lean face were all he needed to be able to tell how close to an explosion they were getting. Or the exact shade of red of the glowing tip of the cigarette that never seemed to be absent from the corner of Louie's mouth. When the high cheekbones shone with an ivory gloss—watch out. When the cigarette end lost its mask of ash and glowed bright cherry-red—duck, fellers, duck.

Smitty, who'd been with Louie longer, claimed he didn't even have to look at *anything*. He claimed he could read certain signs with his eyes shut. Smell them. Hear them.

"There's a kind of sulfur smell in the air," he used to say. "Maybe something to do with the extra hard pull on his cigarette. Faster rate of burning. I don't know. But when I sniff it, then I know. Then I keep very quiet. Very still."

Being a nervy, wiry sort of boy, it took a lot to make Smitty go quiet and still.

"What about the signs you *hear?*" Tim had asked then, wondering if Smitty was putting him on.

"Grinding, mate. A faint gritty grinding. It's his back teeth, I think. That's when he's really getting steamed up. Believe me."

"You must have very sensitive hearing."

"Yer. And very sensitive smell. Very sensitive everything, in fact," Smitty had replied, rolling his big brown eyes. "It's with my mother being Italian. Latin blood."

Well, Latin blood or no Latin blood, Smitty was never wrong. And after a few months, Tim had begun to fancy that he too could read those extra-early warning signs.

So why did those two boys fail to heed them on this particular morning, with Louie's teeth grinding so savagely that they could be heard over the noise of the engine and the rattling of empty bottles behind? With the skin over the cheekbones so tight that it looked ready to split at any moment? With the cigarette end glowing cherry-red and the eyes glinting as bleakly gray as gun muzzles?

Because there was something else in the air besides trouble. That's why.

Something totally different and even more powerful.

Christmas.

The Christmas spirit.

And the reason the boys heard no grinding of teeth was that they were singing. To the tune of "The Twelve Days of Christmas" they were singing about all the extra goodies they'd recently started delivering along with the milk. Today was the day before Christmas Eve. And December 24 was the big delivery day of the whole year. They were limbering up for it. So—instead of partridges in pear trees and lords a-leaping—they were singing of such treats as:

"Fifty cans of peaches!"

"Forty-nine Norfolk turkeys!"

Each boy in turn, really belting it out, closing their eyes the better to hit the right notes—which was probably why they didn't *see* any of the danger signs in the driver's seat beside them.

"Forty-eight *Chrrr*istmas puddings!" sang Smitty, giving it a touch of the old Italian *bel canto*.

"Forty-seven dozen mince pies!" crooned Tim Shaw, remembering his Welsh grandfather and adding a Rhondda lilt.

Just twelve days hadn't been enough for the boys' version. Not with the extra lines *they* had been and would be carrying that Christmas. At any time of the year Louie was noted for the extras he delivered besides milk and cream and the usual dairy things. In summer there would be mushrooms that he picked himself. Fresh vegetables from the garden of an old man who could use the extra money. Shoe repairs, made in the old way, with real leather, by another deserving old-timer. Radio repairs. Watch repairs. Bottles of sherry for old ladies too shy to collect their own. And so on.

But at Christmas that list of extras was more than doubled. Seasonal things mostly. Christmas cheer. Things like:

"Forty-three pounds of sausage!"

"Forty-two special pork pies!"

Louie's cigarette glowed redder and his eyes went bleaker. Not because the boys were messing around with the quantities, just to make the items fit the tune. Oh, no! And not because he objected to singing on the job, either. After all, that day's deliveries had been made. They were on their way back with the empty bottles. No danger of the boys' musical efforts causing any lapse of concentration, errors.

No.

It was because in Louie's book Christmas *was* trouble.

The extra work didn't bother him. Louie thrived on extra work. To him it was a challenge. To him the Spirit of Christmas didn't say any of the usual things like "Be of good cheer!" or "Good will to all men!" To Louie, the Spirit of Christmas seemed to say:

"Huh, well now, they tell me you're the finest milkman in this country—huh—maybe in the whole world, right? . . . All right then—well, now's the time to prove it, buster!"

4

And prove it Louie always had done.

It had been tough going, some years.

In fact, it had been tough going, *most* years.

The trouble was—

Louie broke off his thoughts to wince at a particularly loud bellow from Smitty:

"Thirty-nine three-foot fir trees!"

That was the trouble.

What the Christmas spirit did to his helpers, to their whole frame of mind. Making them too relaxed. Too uppity. Too giggly.

Year after year it was the same. No matter how careful he'd been in selecting them. No matter how many tests he'd put them through. No matter how good and smart and efficient they proved themselves to be during the rest of the year. At Christmas they always became like this. Far too relaxed. And the single word for "far too relaxed" was one of the dirtiest in Louie's vocabulary: *sloppy*.

He nearly choked at the very thought of it. A black dog came trotting out into the road, causing him to swerve sharply. It seemed like just another omen to him.

"Giddout the way!" he snarled—and nearly choked again to see the animal wag its tail in reply, full of the Christmas spirit itself, no doubt. "Ya unhygienic beast, you!"

That sent it slinking off, even if the screech of the truck's brakes hadn't. Louie's voice just then had that sort of note in it—a note that normally would have quieted the boys at once.

But not this day.

Not even that.

Not so near Christmas.

"Thirty-five cans of dog food!" sang Tim, neatly fitting the incident into his carol, reminded of another extra line they'd been carrying lately.

"Thirty-four packs of catnip!" sang Smitty, not to be outdone in the Dumb Friends Department, though this was a pure invention on his part.

Louie ground his teeth.

That was just what he meant. Nothing could shake that mood out of his helpers. There they were, two bright figures in the center of the gathering grayness—Tim with a luminous orange woolen cap tipped jauntily on his yellow hair; Smitty with a bright red woolen cap perched on the back of his dark curls. Still happy. Still full of Christmas good will. Still oozing with potential errors, blunders, slip-ups, misdeliveries, *breakages.*

Louie nearly choked again at the thought of breakages.

But he said nothing.

He knew it was hopeless. Even he couldn't fight this thing. Year after year it had been the same. It had happened with all of them. Hand-picked boys who'd gone on to do great things, thanks partly to the training in thoroughness and efficiency he'd given them.

His mood mellowed a little as he thought of them. There was one who'd become a star actor. There was another who'd become a famous—well, fairly famous—writer. There was an international tennis champion, and a top dress designer.

But they'd all been the same at Christmas.

His eyes went bleak again.

Even those with especially serious minds had been like

this. Even those who'd gone on to be teachers. Even:

> the three eminent lawyers;
> the two politicians;
> and the Mayor of a very large—

Suddenly Louie snarled. He'd caught *himself* doing it! Thinking in tune with these two nuts at the side of him! Reeling off the list of his alumni to the tune of "The Twelve Days of Christmas."

"Belt up, *will* yer! I can't *think* straight. Cut the caterwauling or you'll get out and walk!"

The boys fell silent at last. They knew he meant it. But the quiet soon ended.

"I bet *Scrooge* was a milkman," whispered Tim, forgetting about the sharpness of Louie's hearing even without any Latin blood.

"In that case," growled Louie, just as if Tim had yelled it across the cab, "*I* bet I know why Tiny Tim was a cripple."

"Oh?" said Smitty, genuinely surprised to discover that Louie had read the book.

"Yer!" said Louie, flashing a glare at Tim via the mirror and thereby nearly cracking it. "Too much lip. Too near Christmas."

Again the boys went quiet. But only vocally. For the rest, they were still uppity. Winking at each other. Nudging. Louie could see them . . . fizzing and snorting through their noses. He could hear them . . . shaking with suppressed laughter. He could feel them. . . . For any one of those sins he would have booted them out of the truck, other mornings. But you had to make allowances. Christmas. And at least he could concentrate on his thoughts, with that cats' chorus out of the way.

Christmas . . .

You could have it for him . . .

Besides uppity helpers and having to keep an extra sharp eye on them, Christmas brought other difficulties. It meant coping with customers who went on vacation without remembering to stop their milk deliveries. It meant coping with requests from customers who *had* given warning that they were going away: requests to feed their cats, or simply to keep an eye on their property.

And of course it meant all the extra work tomorrow, the 24th, when two days' deliveries would be crowded into one. There'd be no finishing early tomorrow. They'd be lucky if they were through by early afternoon. Some years they—

"Twenty-six chocolate Yule logs!"

"Twenty-five joints of gammon!"

There they went again. No stopping them.

But Louie was wrong this time. For in the middle of the very next line Smitty did stop.

"Twenty-four—hey! *Mamma mia!* You see what *I* see?"

In his excitement he was twisting this way and that, craning to see out of the windshield and the two side windows.

"Wow! Yes! Oh, *boy!*"

Tim had seen too.

"Yeeargh!"

And so had Louie.

"That's all we"—he coughed over the next word, then

continued—*"need!"*

For this was the biggest trouble yet. This was the biggest lousiest trouble in the smallest prettiest advance packages.

The first snowflakes.

Watching them drift down, the three people saw vastly different things.

The boys saw fun and games. Snowball fights. Toboggan rides.

Tim thought of the snowman he would build for his little sister. Snow*man?* Snow colossus, more like. This year he'd build it ten feet tall, thin but tough, with poles inside to strengthen it, rods of aluminum from the old TV antenna. He'd give it a long thin face, use two beads for its eyes, cut its hair from a sheet of black plastic, smooth and flat with long sideburns, thrust a short white-painted stick in its mouth, light the end, and call it Louie.

Smitty was more artistic. He thought dreamily of the beauties of the snow. The sparkle of frost on the moonlit blanket. Blue shadows on distant drifts. And the miraculous patterns of the tiny single flakes.

But Louie saw none of these things. No fun. No games. No beauties.

All Louie saw was trouble. Blocked streets. Slush. Stalled engines. Skids. Wet socks. Chapped hands. And idiots hiding their empty bottles under two feet of the stuff. Empty bottles containing notes with last-minute requests for cream or eggs or extra milk. Notes that would either get soggy with melting snow, or set hard in their folds with frost. Either way, totally illegible, even if you ever did find them.

"I'm dreaming . . ." began Smitty, leaning out of the window, his crooning mouth open to the sky, eager to taste the first flake.

". . . of a white Chris—" continued Tim.

But he got no further.

Louie had braked sharply.

"You *really* want to walk the rest of the way?"

Louie's eyes were like chips of steel. His cigarette glowed cherry red—but cherry red with blue-white flickers.

This time the Christmas spirit wasn't enough to see them through. This time the nudge that Smitty gave Tim meant "Cool it, fast!"—not "Get *him!*"

"Sorry, Louie," murmured Smitty.

He gave Tim another nudge.

"Yes. Sorry," mumbled Tim.

"You will be," said Louie. "If this stuff keeps coming down."

There were more flakes now. Still not thick and fast, but enough to require the wipers.

Oh, yes!

There was trouble in the air *now,* all right.

But even Louie didn't know just how much until five minutes later, when they reached the dairy.

Chapter Two

The New Helper

"Hello! What's up with *him?*"

As they swung into the yard of New Day Dairies, Louie pulled up short. He had to. Mr. Peters, the manager, was standing there, between them and the main building, waving his arms and looking ready to burst into tears.

"He seems to be waiting for us," said Tim.

"I can see that, you nit!" growled Louie. "But why?"

Smitty gave Tim another cool-it nudge. Only one thing could make the plump little manager stand out in the cold like that, ready to intercept them.

Trouble.

Trouble connected with Louie.

Trouble in the shape of someone already in the building. Trouble that Mr. Peters wanted to damp down if possible, by getting to Louie first.

Smitty had known it happen before.

Once it had been an angry customer. Several times it had been the local Health Inspector, an old enemy of Louie's.

"Well?" said Louie, getting down from the cab.

Already he was rolling up the sleeves of the blue and white sweater he wore, winter and summer alike—the one with the pattern of fighting stags. As he strode up to Mr. Peters, he was scratching his arms, a sure sign that the battle fluids were coursing through his veins.

Mr. Peters stood his ground. His arms had stopped waving about. They were now straight down, palms out, shoulders hunched, in the don't-blame-*me* position. He was wearing his best dark business suit and the snowflakes were already building up on the shoulders and lapels, like dandruff. But that wasn't what was worrying him. On his round face there was an expression that said, as plainly as words, "There are bigger troubles in this world than snow at Christmastime, bad though it might be for the milk trade."

"Well spit it out, man. You look like you've seen a ghost."

"Yes—well—er—now, look, Louie—I—er—now, *please*—"

Any outsider might have been puzzled by this scene. After all, Mr. Peters was the manager, right? And Louie a deliveryman, right? And even a head deliveryman doesn't rate higher than a manager. No?

No.

Most dairies, yes. But this one, no.

Because Louie wasn't just *any* head deliveryman.

Louie was a master. The best. Star quality.

And like stars in other walks of life, Louie didn't see why he should switch from the job he was so good at to one he knew little and cared even less about.

"They don't make star football players into managers while they're still in their prime, do they?" he had said, long ago, when they first tried to promote him. "They don't make star tenors into opera-house managers, just because they're so good at singing?"

The reply could only be, No.

"All right then," Louie had said. "What they *do* do is pay them extra. Let the stars get on with the job they're good at and pay them extra."

And that's the way it had been ever since.

Louie could have been manager ten times over. He was probably earning three times as much as Mr. Peters anyway. Not that he ever bossed Mr. Peters around, taking advantage of his special position. It was just that Mr. Peters knew better than to rile Louie, that was all.

He was trying his best to avoid it now.

"You see, Louie, it—it's like this. I had absolutely nothing to do with it. It's come as just—just as much a surprise to me as—as it has—as it will do—to you."

"What will?"

"This—this new development—"

All the time he was talking, Mr. Peters kept jerking his head over his shoulder toward the office building. His eyes looked hunted. Smitty nudged Tim and gave him a nod. Smitty's money was on the Health Inspector being back there. Maybe some gripe about carrying Christmas trees on the same truck as dairy foods. Tim nodded back.

He had the same feeling too. But what was fascinating him right now was the steam that arose from the mouths and nostrils of each member of the little group out there in the wintry yard.

And no wonder.

Steam is steam, one might say. What difference can it make where it comes from, whose breath it is?

Well, Tim was finding out.

His steam and Smitty's steam, as they stood well to one side, observing all this, was mere *spectator* steam. Like steam from hot dogs. Light puffs.

Mr. Peters' steam, however, was more voluminous, as he stammered out his explanations. Like steam from a pan of simmering cabbage or a dish of milk pudding. Cozy, round, domestic clouds, that hovered before drifting.

But Louie's steam, as he stood there glowering and waiting—that was something else. Jets. Spurts. Plumes. Like steam from the nostrils of an impatient dragon? Closer. Like steam from an ageless Icelandic geyser, jetting up from cracks in bare rock, pressured by millions of gallons of boiling spring water? Closer still.

Most of all, though, it was like steam from a volcano. Thanks to the cigarette, being blown instead of sucked, there were sparks mingling with it. And deep rumblings from behind the battling stags. And the onlookers knew that if there *should* be an eruption, it wouldn't be any mere gush of hot water. No, sir. There would be outpourings of far greater destructive power. Like blinding ash. Like molten lava. Blinding and blasting and petrifying everything that stood near.

The boys took a couple of steps back.

"Now!" rumbled Louie, lighting a new cigarette and looking ready to hurl the old one at Mr. Peters. "Say it.

Tell me. Now. In the next two words. Or so help me—"

"N-new helper!" stammered Mr. Peters, doing just as Louie had asked.

Louie's fist closed over the burning butt end, so that now the sparks were flying from two places at once.

"New WHAT?"

Tim and Smitty took a few further steps back as Mr. Peters came out with it in a rush.

"Just temporary, Louie . . . nothing permanent . . . just a day or two . . . temporary . . . not even helper really . . . more an observer . . . name's Pat . . . Pat Bessemer . . . nice kid . . . I . . ."

Mr. Peters wasn't stammering any more. The gaps between some of his words weren't made by him. They were made inside the head of his chief listener. They were made by the thunder that began to roar in Louie's eardrums— the thunder of rage.

Because this was too much. Even Tim and Smitty were beginning to feel indignant. This was really intolerable, unthinkable. In all the twenty-five years that Louie had been head deliveryman, he had always picked his own boys. That was why he was such a success. (The boys themselves thought so, anyway.)

But actually to thrust some unknown newcomer *onto* him . . .

". . . uncle's Sir Redvers Crump . . . chairman of the whole New Day chain."

Mr. Peters' shoulders slumped. He'd said all he could. He seemed to be hoping that that last bit would see him through in one piece.

"*I* know who the chairman of the company is!" snarled Louie. "What's that got to do with it? Hah? I don't care if he's the Prime Minister of the country. Just because he's chairman doesn't mean he can tell me who—"

"Now listen, Louie, *please!* The kid's an American, a guest, over here on holiday, and—"

"AMERICAN?"

Tim and Smitty took two more steps back.

They knew what this would mean. Louie had views about Americans. Not that he had anything against Americans as such. Far from it. Some of his greatest heroes were Americans. Like Stonewall Jackson, John D. Rockefeller, Eliot Ness. All the flinty, hard-nosed, tough, ingenious, enterprising characters.

"Great country, America," he sometimes used to say. "Shoulda been born there myself."

But where America and *milk delivery* were concerned, it was different.

"Yu-yes, Amer—" began Mr. Peters.

"America's where they're killing off milkmen the way they wiped out the Indians!" howled Louie. "Don't you know *that?* That's where they get their milk in car—car—" Louie wasn't stammering the way Mr. Peters had been stammering. It was another of the dirtiest words in Louie's vocabulary, this next. His mouth revolted at the idea of uttering it. But he made it. ". . . in *cartons!* From soo—soo—" another filthy word coming up—"*supermarkets!*"

Mr. Peters gave another despairing look back at the offices. There were faces at the windows, white blurs behind the steamed glass. Tim wondered which of them belonged to the newcomer.

"But listen, Louie, please. This is an honor. Sir Redvers had so many good things to say about you on his last trip to the States—your efficiency, your training methods, your skill—that the kid can't wait to meet you. In fact—ah!"

It came out as part squeal, part sigh, that last exclamation. It came out just as he had turned his head for another glance back and noticed the slim slight figure in a red parka, black ski pants, and heavy boots, walking out of the office entrance toward them.

Louie was feeling so furious at that point that all he saw was a red and black blur. Otherwise he could hardly have failed to see the warm admiration shining from the large brown eyes as the newcomer advanced.

"Wow!" gasped Smitty, who hadn't missed a thing with *his* large brown eyes.

"Wow! *wow!*" agreed Tim, who saw exactly what Smitty meant.

"I was just telling Louie here how much you've been looking forward to meeting him," babbled Mr. Peters.

"*And* working with him," said the stranger. "I hope you told him that also. Because I sure am. I just can't tell you how pleased I am to meet with you, sir. I begged Daddy and Uncle Redvers to let me do this, and in the end they agreed. Especially when I said it would be the high-spot of my vacation. The best Christmas gift of all."

The warm, clear, honest eyes were smiling from face to face.

Tim and Smitty smiled back.

But Louie was choking again.

Not at the mention of Christmas.

Not at the extra flurry of snow that was coming down.

Not even at the idea of an uninvited helper.

No.

The voice and his clearing vision had suddenly told him that things were getting worse and worse.

For this—the young American—this admirer—this relative of the chairman—this intruder—was a *girl!*

Chapter Three

Pat Makes an Impression

Tim and Smitty had noted the fact much earlier than Louie. Hence, their suddenly oily smiles. Hence, their suddenly standing up taller, shoulders back, chests out, big men. Hence, Smitty's wrinkling his forehead while still grinning, in a way that his Latin blood told him was attractive to women. Hence, Tim's readjusting the tilt of his cap and putting his hands behind his back in an attempt to hide the darn in his left sleeve. (Concerning which his Anglo-Saxon blood suddenly made him fussy and uptight.)

For Pat Bessemer was not only a girl, but a very good-looking one.

"Skin like best double-cream," Smitty was thinking.

"Lips a nice glowing red, like the cap on a bottle of homogenized," Tim reflected.

"Eyes brown but with purplish lights, like the lumps of fruit in black-cherry yogurt," Smitty couldn't help observing.

"Hair that deep gold color, like the foil they wrap best Danish butter in," thought Tim with a gulp, catching sight of a lock that had strayed from under Pat's hood.

But Louie's thoughts were very different.

As with Americans, he had nothing against girls personally. After all, he had the name of one tattooed on his left forearm: JANICE. True, he was scratching at it so vigorously right now that it seemed as if he were trying to erase it, but this was just a coincidence. Janice was still part of his life. He'd been engaged to her for seventeen years, which goes to show. The only reason they'd not got married yet was that she was as dedicated to the dogs at the kennels where she worked as Louie was to his route. They'd just never been able to find the time, is all.

No. Louie had nothing against girls and women. He was even polite to them. When talking to those over forty he always took the cigarette from his mouth. When talking to those of any age he was always respectful. In fact, the quickest way for any of his helpers to get a clipped ear was to be overheard giving lip to a female customer. They say some of the knights of old were like that. Ready to make chopped chicken liver out of any male who so much as gave them a dirty look. But gentle with women at all times. No matter what.

(Even now a change had come upon Louie. The volcano was simmering down. His breathing was still heavy. His scratching was still savage. His eyes still glittered dangerously whenever they glanced at Mr. Peters. But the smell of sulfur had gone.)

So why the inner disturbance, still rumbling away behind the stags?

Because Louie believed that girls had their proper places. In the home. In offices, like Miss Jones over there, just putting her head out of the door. In factories, too, and places like that. In the Army, even. Even in the police force. But not—repeat, *not*—on his route.

In his time at the dairy he'd had nearly two hundred helpers, with never a girl among them. He'd never entertained the idea. He would as soon have signed on with Rely-On-Us Dairies, his detested rivals. And the reason for the all-boys rule, according to Smitty, was: "Discipline."

"Discipline?"

"Discipline, mate. Isn't that the secret of his success? Barking out his orders the way he does. Snap. Growl. Snarl. Girls 'ud never be able to stand it. They'd never understand it. They'd be bursting into tears all the time. *They'd* soon be crying over spilt milk. Specially if they'd done the spilling and Louie caught them at it."

"But Louie would never bawl at a girl."

"Even if she spilled a crate of milk? . . . *Mamma mia,* I wouldn't like to be the girl who risked it! Anyway, Louie knows all this. So he doesn't even take them on in the first place. Unthinkable."

Well, be that as it may, here was Louie now, this cold December morning, faced with the unthinkable in a red parka and black ski pants.

At Christmas, of all times.

With snow in the air.

"Er—yes, Mr. Peters?"

A second female had joined the party. Sylvia Jones, shivering a little in mini-skirt and jumper, was holding a piece of yellow paper. She'd been waiting in the doorway for a signal from the manager, and the yellow paper was what it was all about.

"Is that the telegram?" asked Mr. Peters, as if he didn't know.

She nodded and handed it to him.

Mr. Peters cleared his throat.

"From Sir Redvers himself, Louie," he said, risking a smile. "It reads: 'Please convey my warmest compliments to Mr. Lay and tell him I shall consider it a personal favor—' "

"All right, all right!" Louie was looking fit to erupt again. His cigarette rolled from side to side of his mouth as he spoke. Sparks rose again among the falling flakes. "Fact, it's an order." His voice had that choking quality—always a bad sign. " 'S what you're saying. What it says. Right? An order. I'm being ordered. He's ordering me. Huh? Hah? Right? That it? I'm being ordered to take her with us?"

"I—I'm afraid so, Louie. Yes."

The boys, the manager, and Miss Jones were staring anxiously at Louie. Pat was looking puzzled, as well she might. But those who knew Louie were wondering if this was It. The End. Was he about to pick up his pay and go?

Louie was nodding slowly.

"All right," he said, in a voice that was strangely low. "All right . . ." He looked straight at the manager. "But I'm telling you *this*. I'm warning you *now*. She'll get tret like any other helper." Then he turned and stared hard at Pat. "Chairman's niece or no chairman's niece. Christmas or no Christmas."

It said a lot for Pat that she didn't flinch under that stare. To the contrary, she even managed to smile.

"That suits me, sir," she said. "In fact, I wouldn't have it any other way. No, sir!"

For a fraction of a second, it was Louie who flinched. It was surprise rather than fear, of course. Just a flicker of the eyes.

Then they narrowed, and through the smoke came the rasp of his voice.

"All right then. So the first thing you do is cut out the 'sir' stuff. Just Louie'll do."

Tim glanced at Smitty just as Smitty was glancing at him. Something like amazement was shining in both pairs of eyes. The newcomer might not know it, but she'd just done something no other rookie member had ever come near to doing: caught Louie off guard *and survived*.

Had the shock been too much for him? Had the combination of Christmas, snow, American, and girl been too big an avalanche of troubles? Or was it something to do with the brighter side of Christmas? Had the true Christmas spirit gotten through to him at last, after all these years? Had the true Christmas spirit combined with the fresh good looks of this young girl to create a small miracle, making of Louie a new, kindly, gently good-humored person? Would it all turn out like a late-night movie, with sleigh rides and angel choirs, and Bing Crosby playing the part of Louie? Would—

"WHAT THE DEVIL ARE YOU TWO SMIRKING ABOUT?" came the roar.

And they knew then that whatever else had happened this was still the same Louie and that they, the helpers— all three of them—were in for a Christmas they'd never be likely to forget.

White, it may or may not be.

But it would be stormy. That was for sure.

Chapter Four

Tim Takes a Flip

"Is he always like this?" Pat asked, some fifteen minutes later.

Louie had ordered the boys to stay behind for an extra half-hour or so.

"Seeing how you're so enthusiastic," he had said, "instead of going off home, you can stay and show *her* around. Show her what a milk bottle looks like. Show her how to stack crates. Show her the lot. Then," he had added, with a quick twirl of the cigarette between tight lips—the nearest he ever got to a smile—"then if either of you gets too Christmasy, we can boot you out and she can take your place."

Undeterred by this last threat, the boys had been only too glad to oblige. So they had taken Pat on a tour of the dairy: through the bottling plant and the loading bay, the storerooms, the offices, and finally the head deliveryman's shed. This was Louie's headquarters, across the yard from the main buildings, just the way he wanted it. And it was in here that Pat came out with the question that had been troubling her, ever since her meeting with Louie.

"Is he always like this?"

Smitty jerked his head this way and that, rolling his eyes.

"Like this? Neat, you mean? Orderly?"

He was nodding toward the various items of furniture and equipment in the long narrow room. The table with its neat piles of order books, leaflets, and weekly return forms. The large-scale map of the district on the wall behind the table—marked off into routes, with little red flags sticking here and there, just a few, because these showed where trade was getting slack, and gold flags, many more, because these showed where trade was being improved. The lists: of customers' telephone numbers; of regular specials (customers who gave special orders at regular intervals); and one headed WATCHEMS (customers who were either slow to pay or quick to complain if the milk wasn't left in the shade—things like that).

Even the Christmas cards that Louie had been receiving were displayed with regularity and order, fixed onto strips of Scotch tape and paraded in rows across one of the other walls.

"You *bet* he's always like this," said Smitty.

But Pat was shaking her head.

"No. I didn't mean that. I meant—well, you know—is he always so *mean?*"

"Oh, but he's very generous," said Tim. "He pays us twice as much as the boys at Rely-On-Us Dairies get."

"Yeah, even if we do work three times as hard," said Smitty.

Again Pat shook her head.

"No. I didn't mean *that* sort of mean. I meant the American mean. Growly. Snappy."

"Ah!" said Tim. *"That—"*

"Sister," said Smitty, who'd been practicing an American accent for all he was worth this last fifteen minutes, "when that guy was born they wrapped him up in sandpaper instead of Pampers."

"Yes," said Tim, wanting to make Pat smile himself, "and his first words weren't Momma or Dadda or anything like that. They were—"

" 'Gimmee a light!' " said Smitty, stealing Tim's line. "And he'd been smoking for six months *already!*"

"But don't let that fool you," said Tim, giving Smitty a glare. "He's not bad when you get to know him. He—"

"Naw!" said Smitty. "There's something about him. All his old helpers think the world of him. They all rally round if he's ever in trouble."

"Like last summer," began Tim, "when someone was trying to ruin him by putting things into the milk—"

"He came and gave us a hand," said Smitty, pointing to one of the Christmas cards. "Recognize the face?"

Pat peered at the photograph of a man lifting a champagne glass and winking.

"Isn't that—that's Norbert Rigg, isn't it? The movie star? Don't tell me—"

"That's Nobby all right, sister," said Smitty. "And I *do* tell you. *He* used to be one of Louie's helpers."

"You've met him?"

"Nobby?" said Smitty, as if he were a movie director himself, on first-name terms with every star from Rome to Hollywood. "Sure!"

Pat stared in awe at the photograph and the handwritten inscription under it:

> Always glad to lend you my support, Louie—
> when it's not at the laundry.

She had put out a hand to touch the card from the great actor and this gave Tim his chance. He'd been feeling a bit miffed by Smitty's pushy approach. His Anglo-Saxon blood was a lot slower in circulating around the tongue than Smitty's Latin mixture. But when he saw the bandage on the girl's forearm he took the opportunity to change the subject in a way he could handle better.

"Have you hurt your arm?" he asked sympathetically.

Pat quickly pulled down her sleeve and shrugged.

"Oh, it's nothing," she said. "Just a slight sprain. It's nearly all better now. I got it back home, last week, practicing judo."

"Judo? You? You do judo?"

Smitty had jumped in again. Tim could cheerfully have applied a judo chop to Smitty's neck.

"Sure," said Pat. "At my school everybody gets to learn a little judo."

"Hey!" said Smitty, rolling his eyes toward the window and across at the offices, where they'd last seen Louie. "You ought to tell *him* about that."

"Who?"

"Louie."

"Why?"

"Because he's always getting onto us to learn it. For collecting night. Right, Tim?"

"Right."

"Collecting night?" said Pat.

"Yeah," said Smitty. "When we go round collecting money for the week's supplies. Always a danger of getting mugged, you know."

"Especially in winter," said Tim. "These dark nights."

"But I won't be here on collecting night," said Pat. "Not unless it's tomorrow—"

"No. I *know!*" said Smitty. "But don't you *see? Mamma mia!*" He rolled his eyes at the slowness of his listeners. "You can tell him you're willing to teach *us* a trick or two."

Pat was shaking her head, her lips in a firm line.

"No?" Smitty looked desolate.

"Nuh-huh!"

"You won't teach us?" Now Tim was looking shocked.

"Oh, sure! I'll teach you one or two moves. But I'm not going to tell *him*."

"Why not?"

"Because it'll look as if I'm trying to impress him," said Pat. "And somehow he seems to be the sort of person who's only impressed by what you do, not what you say."

"That's Louie, all right!" said Tim, with a sigh.

Smitty was all a-dither with impatience.

"Yeah, yeh, yeh! But you *will* teach us?"

"Sure."

"Now? Right now?"

Pat shrugged. The room was nice and large, with plenty of bare floor space.

"If you like. Yes. . . . Do you want to try first, Smitty? Try and jump on me from behind. Come on."

Suddenly Smitty's eyes rolled faster than ever.

He backed away a pace.

"Hey . . . now hold it . . . I didn't mean *exactly* now, right here, this very minute . . ."

"What's the matter?" asked Pat "I know how to throw you so you won't get hurt. Just shook up maybe, but not hurt."

This time Tim really did see himself in with a chance. When it came to words, Smitty could waste him. But deeds were something else. . . .

"*I* will," he said.

"Go on, then," said Pat, turning her back. "And do it as if you really meant it. Try and put an arm around my neck as if to choke me."

"You sure?"

"Sure."

"Your arm—?"

"Forget it. I won't even need to use it."

Well, Tim didn't go into the move flat out. But then again he didn't play it too gentle. After all, the girl wouldn't want him to do that. She wanted to prove how good she was and he didn't want to make her look foolish. So he decided he'd put just enough beef into it to show he was no softy, and then *pretend* to be caught in one of her holds.

Like this . . .

He stepped forward quickly. One, two, three, and . . .

Kerash!

There was no pretending about the thud with which he landed flat on his back. Just as there'd been no pretending about the sudden lift-off and glide—beautifully flighted, brilliantly controlled—over Pat's left shoulder.

Nor—if it comes to that—was there any pretending about the menace in the voice that suddenly rasped over his head with a blast of cold air from the doorway:

"I thought you'd come here to *look round* the place, not break it up!"

Louie. Cheekbones white.

"Sorry, sir!"

Pat. Cheekbones red.

"She was showing us some judo holds, Louie. Ain't that something? She—"

Smitty faltered to a stop as Louie flicked him a glance.

"Where you staying?" he said, addressing Pat again.

"With Mr. and Mrs. Peters."

"Well, get off there and get some rest," snapped Louie. "They told you what time we start in the morning? . . . Right. . . . You two. Same. Get off home. And I did say *rest*. You're gonna need to be fit tomorrow if this lot"—he jerked his head at the window, and ash fell from his cigarette like a reflection of the snowflakes outside—"keeps on. And even if it doesn't," he added grimly, "you'll still need to be extra fit, what with double deliveries"—he paused—"and a passenger to carry."

Pat flushed. For the first time, her smile wobbled. Then her eyes blazed. But she tightened her lips and turned.

"Right," said Louie, going to his desk and sitting down.

"That settles that." He paused as he reached for a pile of order books and looked up at the boys. "Well? What you waiting for?"

Smitty grinned. He'd been secretly practicing the famous Norbert Rigg wink for days. He had a sudden urge to put it into operation and answer Louie's question with a single word, "Christmas."

But then he caught the full blast of the famous Louie Lay scowl and thought better of it.

Without another murmur, he followed the others out into the gently falling snow.

Chapter Five

Louie Under the Stars

The cat looked up with wide frightened green eyes.

It was a black cat. It had found itself a dry corner at the side of its house, a corner from which the snow had been swept. By contrast, the shadows there were deeper than ever. Black as the cat itself. A perfect hide-out until the dawn.

Or so the animal had figured.

But just now it was beginning to wonder. Just now, at 3:45 A.M. on the morning of December 24, it was beginning to wonder if giants had begun to walk the earth again.

Menacing giants from whom no one—cat or human—would ever be safe.

Tall. Thin but tall. Immense against the stars, it blacked them out, constellation by constellation, as it strode nearer. Tall and thin, forked like a man, legs like a man. Tall and thin and two-legged, but with black shadowy bumps and projections jutting from its body. Tufts and tails and sproutings such as the cat had seen on no man before.

Nor was this all that terrified the cat.

As the shape got nearer, a single bright-red twitching eye could be seen through the clouds of mist around the head. And, as if that wasn't alarming enough, strange sounds came wheezing and barking and grunting from the region of that eye. Inhuman sounds.

The cat shuddered and crouched further into the corner . . .

Louie knew nothing about this silent watcher. To him, it seemed as if he were the only one around on the streets just then. After all, this was a good half-hour earlier than his normal appearance. Usually he was striding along to the dairy for a 4:30 start, ready to put in a solid two hours' work before his helpers met up with him, along the route. Today, however, was different.

He would still be starting at 4:30, but there was more to attend to by way of preliminaries. More extras to make sure had been loaded properly. More extra-extras to find spaces for in whatever nooks and crannies the loaders had left him. And, because it was a school holiday, Tim and Smitty would be joining him at 4:30 instead of 6:30. Or they'd better be.

So there, straight off, was the answer to all the cat's

bewilderment concerning the strange lumps and bumps that jutted from Louie's silhouette. The *extra*-extras. Things like the two long narrow trays of Cumberland rum butter —just the thing for spreading on Christmas puddings and a great favorite with some of Louie's more discerning customers. Made according to a special recipe handed down through the generations from Bonny Prince Charlie's chief cook, and now owned by Louie's Aunt Ada. Great stuff, that Cumberland rum butter, and at ten pence an ounce the bargain of the year.

Also, swelling his pockets or billowing under his sweater, tucked under his arms or hanging from his belt, were (just to name a few more extra-extras):

> a set of colored lights, second-hand but only used once, still in the original presentation box;
> a quart jar of elderberry wine, home-made by a cousin of Janice's;
> three giant-size Christmas stockings, stuffed with candies, small tin toys, picture books, and fortune cookies;
> two boxes of assorted cake decorations;
> two large holly wreaths, red-ribboned and frosted (ringing his shoulders, one at each side, Louie having threaded his arms through them).

None of this last group had been ordered specially by anyone. But Louie knew what he was doing. These were just the kinds of things that people ran out of at Christmastime at the very last minute. Finishing touches. Small gifts for unexpected guests. And, just when some of his customers would be kicking themselves for having forgotten, along would come Louie to save the day.

Service.

It did him good to think about it.

"Two jumps ahead, that's me!" he thought—thereupon taking the equivalent of four jumps ahead as he slid on a chunk of loose ice, headed for the dark corner, and nearly scared the cat out of its skin.

But he righted himself in time. There was hardly a pause as he resumed his thoughts and the strange low bellowings and honkings that had so disturbed the cat earlier.

Singing seems hardly the word.

Yet that's what the noises were.

For (and this is a great secret) Louie did sometimes sing. Only when he felt he was completely alone, mind you. And only when he felt extremely happy. At such times, his face never changed much. The eyes remained beady. The mouth remained tight-lipped around the cigarette. But he did sing.

Well—*sing* . . .

Maybe that's not the right word after all.

He thought it was singing. He could even have told you the name of the song.

"Tom Dooley."

It was the only one he knew. And of the words, the only two he was completely sure of were *Tom* and *Dooley*.

So he ought to be given the benefit of the doubt.

Anyway, what had seemed to the cat to be the inhuman grunting of an alien spirit, and what seemed to some householders turning in their sleep to be the dying cries of a sick dog, was, in reality, just this:

"Yerrum hah haff HOM HOOLEH,

　Yerrum kra kaff hum coch,

　Yerrum hah haff HOM HOO-ELLEH,

　Yerrum kitch kruff cum frabb!"

And why was Louie so pleased?

After all those forebodings and shocks of the day before, why was he moved to sing on his way to work, that morning?

Because his greatest fears had turned out to be unfounded.

The snow had behaved itself.

It had fallen steadily for several hours yesterday, true, but in the most co-operative manner possible, mainly in the middle of the afternoon. Thanks to this, the traffic had been able to crush it out of existence on all the important streets of the town even as it was falling. What remained —on certain sidewalks, roofs, and walls—was no more than two inches deep in any one spot. And, best of all, even before the end of the afternoon, the clouds had drifted away, leaving a perfectly clear sky that looked set to remain that way for at least another forty-eight hours.

Louie peered up at it now.

Not a wisp of cloud.

Nothing to obscure a nice three-quarters moon, still fairly high, to light them on their route for the first few hours. And millions of stars.

Louie tore off another two verses of "Tom Dooley" as he strode on, squinting up at the constellations.

The Great Bear, the Plow, the Seven Sisters, the Ram

—he knew them all. Not by those names, though. Louie was no astronomer, even if he did know where to get a good reliable cheap telescope for any customer who should fancy one. No. But when you have so many twinkling points to work on, it's not difficult to join them up into any shapes you care to think of. Therefore, it was *his* constellations that Louie looked up at that morning. The shapes *he* cared to think of. His old friends the Large-Size Yogurt and the Empty Crate, the Seven Half-Pints and the Churn.

So, what with the single bright one he always thought of as the Double Cream directly ahead of him, and what with all those last-minute gifts strewn around his body, it was no wonder that Louie felt a bit like the leader of the Three Wise Men as he entered the gates of the New Day Dairy.

Then he saw the light shining in the window of his shed—his own headquarters! already! before he'd got there! —and all such gentle musings left him.

"If it's burglars," he muttered, "I'll belt 'em with this jar of wine!"

He stopped. The main building was in darkness, just as his shed should have been. The only lights that had any right to be on at this moment were over in the loading bays and the bottling plant, shining through the billows of steam like the lights of a ship preparing for an early tide.

Louis moved on, softly now, stealthily.

"And if it's one of the night-shift loaders snooping around," he promised himself, as he reached out a hand and lifted a foot, ready to open the shed door with a kick,

"I'll wrap these Christmas holly wreaths round his neck, ribbons an' all!"

But it was neither burglar nor snooping workmate.

As he booted open the door, prepared to pounce, he was arrested by a stifled scream and another pair of wide frightened eyes. Not green eyes this time, though. Brown ones. With purple depths.

It was Pat.

Chapter
Six

Louie
Under Fire

Out under the stars, Louie had looked frightening enough to the cat. But here, in the light of the shed, he was an absolutely terrifying sight.

The wreaths were still around his shoulders. Huge prickly humps with the ribbons flowing down, one over his ear and across his face, like rivulets of blood.

The two long plastic-wrapped trays of Aunt Ada's Cumberland rum butter were tucked under the right arm. In that position, jutting out and up, they looked more like a brace of interplanetary death-ray projectors.

The big white cotton-net Christmas stockings were suspended from Louie's belt, under the sweater. To Pat just then they looked like three extra legs, or feelers. The bright greens and reds of the gifts inside them did nothing to reassure the girl, either. They suggested that this was the creature's basic flesh color—mottled, marbled, metallic.

Worst of all, perhaps, was the sight of the quart jar of elderberry wine, raised high in the intruder's right hand and obviously ready to be brought swinging down on someone's head.

Not at all pleasant at four o'clock on a midwinter morning, when you are that someone.

But, of course, it was all over very rapidly. A quick look at the freshly shaved morning face of Louie, sporting a freshly lighted morning cigarette, convinced the girl that all was well. Normally that face—with its glittering eyes and strangely scarred cheeks, nicked in places by razor and frost—might itself have given her a stab of alarm. But after those first impressions it came as sweet relief.

"Oh, it's you, sir!" she said.

Louie too seemed relieved, though this was shown only in the lowering of the wine jar.

"Yer!" he growled. "It's me. Without the sir, don't forget." He peered at her suspiciously. "You been on the night shift?"

She was now fully recovered. She was smiling again. She was secretly proud of having got there before Louie. None of his helpers had ever done *that* before, either.

"We believe in getting up early where I come from," she said.

"Oh, yer? . . . How did you get here this morning?"

"Mr. Peters. He brought me in his car."

Louie's cigarette twirled. She didn't know it but she'd just achieved another first. Getting him to grin like that. But then, of course, she didn't recognize it *as* a grin.

"You mean you got him out of his bed, this time the morning?"

She nodded, wondering. Had she said something wrong? What did that savage twirling of the cigarette mean? She would have to ask Tim and Smitty, she decided.

"Well," she said, uncertainly, "when he heard I was starting so early, he offered."

Louie nodded.

"Yer. Suppose it was all he *could* do."

He could understand Mr. Peters' predicament. When the niece of the chairman of the whole company is staying with you, you do your best to please. If she wanted to play mud-pies in the bathroom, you'd go along with it. You'd help to carry the buckets of earth upstairs. Yes. Wasn't Louie *himself* breaking all his old rules by letting her come on the route?

All the same, the idea of the plump little manager having to drive to the dairy so early tickled Louie. Mr. Peters usually started at 8:00 A.M.—early enough for an office worker, sure, but really the middle of the afternoon to Louie.

His cigarette twirled again. Twice.

For two pins he could have honked out a chorus of "Tom Dooley."

Then he noticed something different about the shed and scowled.

"Wass 'at, then?" he rumbled, giving the wine jar a menacing underarm swing toward the far corner.

On the floor over there was a small circular electric heater. And the reason why Louie didn't recognize it as such at once was that it was the dual-purpose type. The sort that doubled as a portable cooker when laid flat on its back.

It was in that position now, with a pan of water bubbling on top of it.

"Oh, *that!*" Again Pat smiled. "I borrowed it from Mrs. Peters. I thought you and the boys might like a cup of coffee before you started. It's only instant, I'm afraid, but—"

"What d'you think we're *on?*" snapped Louie. "A church outing?" Then, as the idea got through to him, he eased off some. "Go on, then," he said, putting down the wine jar at last.

Gladly, Pat set to, heaping the powder into one of the beakers she'd also borrowed.

"How d'you like it?"

"Black an' boilin'," grunted Louie. "Thanks."

Yet another first. That "thanks" as he took the steaming beaker. But then, none of his helpers had ever been a female before now.

Pat felt she was winning hands down.

And she still had her ace to play.

She decided to go ahead.

"And I've checked out with the weather forecast. On the telephone."

Louie looked up sharply. That in itself should have warned her.

"Oh?"

"Yes," she said, still feeling on top of the world. "And they say there's a chance of snowstorms later this morning."

"'Chance'!" Louie snarled. "Why they always say *chance?* Never *risk?* Oh, no! Never *danger.* Never *danger* of snowstorms. No. *Chance.* As if we're all lookin' forward to it!"

Then Pat made it even worse. She'd always been taught to see both sides of an argument. To give them both a fair hearing at all times. So she put the case for the opposition.

"Well, some people *are* looking forward to it, I guess."

Louie glared at her. Then,

"Yer!" he said, slowly. "And there's a *chance* that *some people'll* be out there working till midnight because of it. Thank you very much!"

This last "thank you" didn't rate. Even Pat could tell that, from the way he gritted it out.

Then he snatched the cigarette from his mouth, gulped down the still hot liquid without twitching an eyebrow, and stomped out of the shed.

Poor Pat!

For about half a minute she stared at the door wondering what she'd done or said wrong *this* time.

And she was just trying to reassure herself that a girl can't win 'em all when the door swung open again and the boys came in.

Tim's eyes seemed to be closed still. He was moving like a zombie—slow, stiff, mechanical. But Smitty was as chirpy as ever.

"Where is he, then? Hey, there's a good smell in here!

How d'you like staying with Old Peters? Is it true his wife smokes a pipe? Well, where is he?"

"Mr. Peters?"

"Naw! Old Lou Scrooge . . ."

"Over at the loading bay, I think."

"Hah! Well. Wait till—hey, steady, boy!" Smitty broke off to steer the swaying Tim to a chair. "Don't mind him," he said to Pat. "Never fully conscious till seven. . . . No. Louie. Wait till he sees these!"

Smitty was digging deep into the pockets of his duffel coat. A pleasant soft rattling sound came from them. Then he pulled out two handfuls of chestnuts, brown and bright as his rolling eyes.

"Another last-minute extra," said Smitty. "Dee-lishious! Just the job for turkey stuffing. Parcel arrived yesterday. All the way from Italy. We'll be able to sell 'em like hot cakes. . . . Chesta-nuts! Roasted chesta-nuts!"

As Smitty went into his act, Pat turned to the yawning Tim.

"Want some coffee? You look as if you need it."

"Uh—yuh—yeeow—yes. Yes, please."

But before she could get the pan back on the heater, Smitty had bustled her away.

"Hey! This gives me an idea. Quick. Mind out of the way . . ." He had already picked up the large can lid that Louie used as an ash tray for his desk. Now he placed it on the red-hot circle of heat. "There!" he said, spilling out a fistful of chestnuts onto the lid. "Now we can-a really have-a da roast chestnuts!"

The others stared with approval. Smitty could be forgiven everything for that idea. Even his bustling around at this unearthly hour. Even his mock Italian accent, for which his mother would surely have given *him* a roasting if she'd heard.

So they sat around chatting, waiting for Louie and waiting for the nuts to roast—and hoping that the latter would be first. And once again Pat was feeling glad to have come to this place, hairy though the experience had looked like being from time to time. Even so, she was growing cautious.

"But aren't you supposed to go help him with the last-minute loading?" she asked, not wanting to be blamed for keeping the boys talking.

"Nuh-huh!" said Smitty, who had caught that expression off Pat already. "We're never here this early, so there's no fixed routine."

"Plenty—ooh-yow!—" yawned Tim, "plenty of routine when we're delivering though. You'll see—" He blinked at his watch. "Nearly time, anyway. You'll—"

Tim broke off.

Not for another yawn, though. Oh, no! Not this time.

In fact, the two things that caused him to break off right then, also caused him to spring to full consciousness a good three hours before the time predicted by Smitty.

These two things came almost exactly together.

One: Louie pushed open the door and snapped, "What d'you think this—?"

Then he too broke off. Because Thing Number Two happened at precisely that moment. Or should it be Things Number Two through Fifty-Two? Or One Hundred and Fifty-Two?

Anyway, what sounded like a fusillade from a firing

squad suddenly crackled out, and they all ducked as bits of blazing hot chestnut flew around the room.

The three helpers ducked, anyway.

Louie's nerves were better.

His temper wasn't so good, mind you, but you have to hand it to his nerves.

He just stood there. Glaring.

An extra-large hunk of chestnut must have come close to knocking his front teeth out. As it was, it had damaged his cigarette, bending the end and breaking the paper, so that it now glowed but feebly.

There was nothing feeble about the light in his eyes, however. Especially the right one, with a spattering of yellow nut kernel still clinging to the brow above it.

"Su-sorry, Louie!" stammered Smitty. "I forgot. You should crack the shells first before—"

"OUT!"

Not quite a roar, but more than a growl.

They got up and moved.

"Out! All of yer! Before I crack *your* shells!"

And did Smitty get the fiercest glare for being the one who had brought those stinking lousy chestnuts? (Pat was beginning to feel mad herself now.)

Oh, no!

That glare was reserved for Pat.

"He as good as said it!" she muttered indignantly, as they trooped out under the stars behind Louie, to the loading bay and the waiting truck.

"Said what?" asked Tim.

"Said it was my fault for bringing the heater."

"Argh, forget it!" said Smitty. "He'll get over it. Besides, it's that weather report that really got under his skin."

"Yes!" said Pat. "And just because I was the one to tell him about it, I'm blamed for *that,* also."

But she'd show him, she thought, fuming.

Yes, sir, but she'd show him.

Chapter
Seven

The Problem—
and Tubby Hooley's
Golden Answer

Maybe Pat would not have been quite so sore if she'd known what was on Louie's mind that morning. Maybe her sense of fairness would have helped her to understand his uptightness better.

For Louie certainly had problems.

None of them was easy, but the main one, that day, was a stinker—and it was this:

He had two days' deliveries to make at every customer's house on the route. So he could either (1) cover half the route on the first trip, making his double deliveries, then go back to the dairy, load up again, and cover the other half on a second trip; or (2) he could cover the whole route as usual, making a single day's delivery at every house, then go back, load up, and cover it all again later in the day.

Sometimes, when he was hiring new helpers, he'd set this problem as one of the tests.

"Which would *you* choose?" he would ask the candidates. "Write it down—(1) or (2)—and say why."

Some boys picked (1), pointing out that it saved gas because the truck would be covering less distance even if it did have to go slower.

Some boys picked (2), pointing out that every customer on the route would get at least part of his supply early in the morning, when it counted. Working on Method 1 would mean that some customers would be without milk until late in the afternoon.

Which was right?

Many of those candidates, successful or not, still argue about it to this day—even those who are grown-up and have families. Fights have been known to break out because of it. And some of Louie's alumni are not on speaking terms because they can't agree.

Louie never steps in to settle it. In his view, neither (1) nor (2) is better than the other. To him, all that matters is the reason a boy gives. If he talks about gas consumption and distances it shows he has a good practical intelligence. If he talks about the customer's point of view it shows he has a good sense of service to the public. Either way, he's still in the running, ready to go on to other tests. Only when he gives no good reason, just guesses, is a boy flunked at that stage.

At the back of Louie's mind there is, of course, an ideal answer, the Golden Answer, the giving of which would get a boy hired straight away. Only one has ever given it—a kid called Tubby Hooley, who went on to become one of Britain's greatest lawyers. This is what he wrote:

> Number One is the better method. It saves fuel because considerably less distance is covered. Admitted, customers on the second half will have to wait longer, but a good milkman will notify them well in advance, so that they can keep a little extra milk back to see them through the morning.

Louie's cigarette made five consecutive twirls, the day he got that answer.

But young Tubby wasn't through even then. When he saw that Louie had read his answer and had appreciated the reasoning, he said, "There's just one extra point I'd like to add, however. Assuming this double-delivery problem arises at Christmastime, and further assuming the weather is inclement—"

"Eh?" said Louie, and no wonder, for that was just the way Tubby talked even as a kid.

"Snow," said Tubby.

"Ah!" said Louie.

"Well, in that case it depends when the main snowfall has occurred. If it has already occurred, Method One is still the better, because whichever you pick you'll still have the same additional difficulties. But if—am I going too fast for you?"

"No. Go on. It was just the mention of snow."

"But if the snowfall should occur in the *middle* of the day, there could be a danger in Method One."

"You said it!" grunted Louie, two jumps ahead already.

"It could be so heavy that any further deliveries would be impossible. Therefore *all* the customers on the second half would be left without any milk at all. Whereas if you'd used Method Two and been round to them all, before the snow got too bad, at least they'd have *some* milk."

"Sonny," said Louie, giving his cigarette another five twirls, "you're in. When can you start?"

All that is ancient history, of course. It happened years before Pat and Tim and Smitty were born. And in all those years Louie had never been stuck with such a tricky situation. Blizzards had come before Christmas, blizzards had come after Christmas. But never had one come at the critical time mentioned by Tubby—slap in the middle of the day, with Louie already committed to Method One.

Now, however, the dread occurrence looked like hitting them, according to the forecast that Pat had passed on to him. And the truck was already loaded with the exact requirements of the customers on the first half of the route: all the regular orders, all the specials, all the extra-specials. It would take too long to unscramble it all now. Louie would just have to press on and hope for the best.

No wonder he was worried.

Already, as he revved up the engine and glanced at the sky, the first clouds were crossing the stars, blotting out the Churn and cutting the Seven Half-Pints to Three.

Chapter
Eight

Pat
Is
Impressed

The first deliveries began only a few blocks from the dairy.

This was a good thing. It was, in fact, a very good thing indeed. In fact, the chances are that Pat—certainly Pat—and maybe Tim and Smitty too—might have been ordered out of the cab if the first deliveries hadn't started so soon.

Why?

Well, figure it out. Picture it yourself. Two bright growing boys. Full of the Christmas spirit. One of them dead on his feet a few minutes ago through being up so early, granted—but now as alert and lively as the next boy, thanks to that fusillade of chestnuts.

So there they are. Starry morning. Moonlight. Christmastime. A nice crisp layer of snow already and the promise, the *chance* (never mind what Louie thought), the delightful possibility of more to come.

Then top it all up with a girl. A bright good-looking girl like Pat. An *American* girl, too—the sort that didn't come their way every week. Put that girl in the cab with them, that Christmas Eve morning, under the stars (there were still plenty to be seen, in spite of the clouds), squeeze that girl into the cab with them, *sit her on their knees* (Smitty's right and Tim's left)—and what do we get?

We get whisperings and nudgings, that's what. We get gleeful murmurings and gulped-back giggling. We get something that reminded Pat—in spite of the cold—of the beginning of a hayride she'd once gone on, back on her grandfather's farm in Vermont.

Oh, yes! No doubt about it. Had that first stretch of the journey been any length at all, Louie—sitting there in the darkness with his cigarette glowing like the fuse of a bomb—Louie would have blown up.

But as soon as the truck stopped, discipline took charge. Real discipline. The self-discipline that comes from thorough drill and first-class training. Louie didn't have to blow up. He didn't even have to grunt or snarl. Not even in an undertone. All he did was get out of the cab on his side and the rest automatically followed.

Out jumped Smitty on *his* side of the cab, and one half of Pat went down with a bump. Then out jumped Tim on Louie's side, and the other half of Pat went down with a bump. And before she knew what had happened, Smitty was already delivering two pints of homogenized on his first doorstep, Tim was bustling with his handcrate to the first of his customers across the street, and Louie was assembling all the specials and extra-specials for the whole block.

"You just watch," he said to Pat as she stuck her head out. "Watch all you want, but don't get in the way."

For Louie, the order came out quite mildly. That was his way when he was actually working and nothing was going wrong. He was far too efficient a deliveryman to waste his energy bawling people out merely from habit.

So that is what Pat did at first. Watched. And was glad to. It was so fascinating. She had expected great things from Louie and his team. But this was even better. Under the circumstances—the poor light and the layout of those streets—it was little short of miraculous.

For this was one of the poorest parts of the town. And the poorest part of a British town tends to be very different from the poorest part of an American town. Back home, there would have been tenements, run-down apartment buildings. Here there wasn't anything over two stories. Instead there were rows and rows of little houses without yards. And these rows were not at all straight, set out in regular blocks, in good sensible American patterns. No. They were choppy. They were broken up by irregular cross streets. Some of these were short cul-de-sacs. Some of them curved away in crescents. Some opened out into dark pocket-handkerchief squares.

A maze. That's what it was in Pat's eyes, as she blinked

around. A warren. A crazy network. To her, at first, it seemed a miracle that Louie and the boys ever found their way around, let alone made their complicated deliveries so quickly and surely.

But then, as the truck nosed its way along from one point to the next, she began to pick out the pattern. Not the pattern of the streets down there, of course. That would have taken weeks. But the pattern of the way Louie's system worked.

Like this:

The truck would be parked at a strategic point—usually at an intersection of several streets; always under a street light. From this point, Louie and the boys would hustle off with small handcrates, each of which held a dozen bottles, with extras like cream or orange juice tucked away somewhere between their tops. Then, even before Pat had time to decide which of the three to follow, back they would come, faster than they had gone, the handcrates bright with lightly jingling empties.

Then—flash, flick, clash, clish—the empties would be plucked from the handcrates and transferred to larger crates on the truck. And—flash, flick, clash and clish again (in a lower key but with a brighter flash)—into the handcrates would go more full bottles.

The boys, Pat noted, always had farther to go than the man. They would disappear, into the shadows at the end of a street, around corners, down alleys; whereas Louie always stayed near the truck, delivering at houses within sight of it.

"*Lazy* old Louie!" Pat thought at first, thinking she'd caught him out and feeling rather pleased.

But no.

She soon had to admit she was wrong.

The way he moved, he managed to deliver almost as much as both boys together. And the reason for his keeping the truck in sight was soon apparent. It was so that he should be in a better position to mastermind the whole miracle. To answer any queries. To find any last-minute extras that might be required. And constantly to keep the truck tidy—making sure that crates for empty bottles were always available, and that those already filled with empties were shoved out of the way. On a truck as heavily loaded as that, this juggling about with crates and spaces was no easy task. This time, Pat was reminded of those puzzles where little numbered squares have to be pushed around, with only one space free at any one time, until they end up in correct order: 1 through 15.

That was the pattern of the way they worked.

Mind you, it wasn't until they'd been on the route a good half hour, still in the warren of poor streets, that the girl managed to sort it out. At first it was all confusion—a confusion of sights and sounds.

Blinking from one to another of them, trying to keep track of Tim's orange cap, or the bright red pom-pom on Smitty's, or the glow of Louie's cigarette, her head began to whirl, forcing her to close her eyes from time to time. Then it would be just sounds, just as confusing.

The crunch and squeak of boots on frosty snow. The snap of Louie's heels on the cleared stretches of sidewalk. The grunted queries and commands.

"Two more double-creams at Twenty-five."

"Catch!"

"Did you say Thirty-three canceled last night, Louie?"

"Yer. How many more times?"

"Another four silver-tops."

"Where's all the gold-tops gone, Lou?"

"Starin' at yer, ya mug!"

"Catch!"

"Hey—watch it!"

And so on. Interspersed with the soft clash of glass on metal, the heavier clash of crate on crate, the rhythmic chink-chink into the shadows. Then the revving of the engine, ready to move on, and the gritty sliding of the doors.

"Hutch up a bit! Can't find my gears for feet!"

"Sorry, Lou!"

"And shut that door properly, will yer!"

Not angry remarks. Just routine mutterings. The sound of experts—sweet as music—synchronized, harmonious, no longer confusing.

A very special Christmas carol, thought Pat.

Chapter Nine

The First Calamity

Pat's next big wave of interest came between 5:30 and 6:00, with the first appearances of other people: early-rising customers, other deliverymen, newspaper boys. By now the moon was masked completely, just a lighter blur through the thickening clouds—a blur with a faint rainbow halo, as if in honor of Christmas. But compensating for this was the extra light from various house windows, as people began to get up.

The customers sometimes appeared at bedroom windows.

"Don't forget my extra eggs this time," one woman called down, shivering a little in the raw air.

"Sorry, lady," said Louie. "You got the wrong firm."

"Isn't that Rely-On-Us Dai—oh!" The woman stuck her head out farther, blinking. "I thought it was the Rely-On-Us van."

"*This* time of the morning?" jeered Smitty. "You'll not see that mob till the streets are aired. And even then—"

"Shaddap!" said Louie softly. "The lady's new here. Let her find out for herself."

All the way to the next delivery point, Louie gave Smitty a lecture about knocking the competition.

"Never do it. Hear? How many more times I got to tell yer? Folks don't need us to tell 'em how lousy Rely-On-Us are. Let 'em find out the hard way."

"Besides, is it *fair?*" said Pat.

Louie gave her a scowl.

Pat stuck to her guns.

"I mean what Smitty was saying. About the other firm being late. That's one of their trucks now, isn't it?"

It was. It was just starting up in a cloud of steamy pollution, at the side of the curb ahead.

As the New Day truck went past, a jeer arose from the rival cab.

"Whata loada rubbish! Whata loada rubbish!"

Chanted. Derisive. Pat had heard the same chant a few days earlier on British television: a crowd at a soccer game.

Smitty leaned out. He began a chant of his own.

"Rely-On-Us and get left in the—"

Zapp!

Across the faces of Pat and Tim came Louie's left arm. And—zapp!—back it went, yanking with it Smitty's head from the window.

"Mind yer mouth!" snapped Louie. "We got a young lady on board, don't forget!"

"I wasn't gonna say nothin' *bad!*" protested Smitty. "I was only gonna say, 'Rely-On-Us and get left in the *slush!*'"

"Neh mind that!" grunted Louie. "I know you. You get carried away."

In the darkness of the cab, Pat felt herself glowing almost as warmly as Louie's cigarette.

"'A young lady'!" he'd growled.

It was the first nice thing he'd said about her. From anyone else it wouldn't have been much. From anyone else she might even have resented it. She never had cared much for that expression. Usually when people addressed her as "young lady" it was to open up a scolding. Or at least a nagging.

But from Louie—

Wow!

She felt so good about it that she even defended him against the next customer to stick her head out of a bedroom window.

"Hoy!"

Big woman. Fat face. Hair bristling with steel curlers. Japanese-type dressing gown. Cigarette out of the side of *her* mouth, too.

"That you, Lay?"

"Yer. 'S me, Mrs. Perkins. We left the extras you ordered."

Louie had taken his cigarette out to reply, Mrs. Perkins being well over forty.

"Also, she's a right complainer!" Smitty whispered.

"Even Lou treads carefully with *her*."

"You'd *better* of left the extras I ordered," said the woman.

"Yer, well, I think you'll find—"

"It's not that I'm inquiring about. It's *that!*"

Mrs. Perkins plucked the cigarette out of the side of her mouth and stabbed it down in the direction of the street. They looked around. At least the boys and Louie did. Pat just stared back up. The cigarette seemed to be pointing right at her. Straight between the eyes.

"That's a girl, en' it?" said Mrs. Perkins. "That's a girl you got down there helping you, en' it?"

"Well, yer—but—"

"Never mind your 'buts,' Louie Lay. That *is* a girl. Yet when my own Alice once went for a job with you, you told her you never hired girls. Poor kid, she came back sobbing her little heart out!"

"*Little* heart?" murmured Smitty. "Big fat Alice Perkins?"

Luckily Mrs. Perkins didn't hear that. She was too busy working herself up into a rage.

"So now you changed your mind, huh?"

"That was years ago, Mrs. Perkins. That—"

"What? Hey? Hah? You saying I'm an old hag, Lay? You *insulting* me now?"

Mrs. Perkins looked in two minds: undecided whether to come down and tackle Louie on the doorstep, or take a header out of the bedroom window—curlers, cigarette, Japanese gown and all—and crush the four of them in one kamikaze dive.

Meanwhile, other lights were going on. Growls of protest were floating down from unintended early risers.

"Now listen, Mrs. Perkins," said Louie. "She isn't even a helper. She—"

"What's she doing there then?"

"She—"

"I'm an observer," said Pat, in her clearest tones. "I've come over here to write about this wonderful delivery operation for a big American magazine."

Well. It wasn't totally untrue. Pat did intend to write about her experience. And although *The Ward Ridge Girls School Student Monitor and Gazette* may not have been a big magazine to *some* Americans, to the editor and its contributors it certainly was.

Mrs. Perkins' jaw dropped, and the replaced cigarette drooped with it.

"Go on!" she said—and her voice was vibrant with curiosity now, not rage. "Is that so?"

"Sure!"

"You really are American?"

"As apple pie, ma'am."

"And—"

"Mrs. Perkins," said Louie, respectfully, "maybe some other time. We still have a lot of deliveries to make."

"That's true, ma'am. And I do have to get on with my observing."

"Just one question," Mrs. Perkins called out, as they were about to get back in the cab.

"Ma'am?" said Pat.

"During your observations, you see anything *they* do that a girl couldn't?"

Pat hesitated. Then decided on the truth.

"Not a thing, ma'am."

Mrs. Perkins smirked.

"Right then. You see you put *that* in your article. And you tell your readers about my Alice. If you want a photo-graph—"

Pat felt the back of her parka being plucked by a firm hand.

"Git *in!*" growled Louie, letting in the clutch with his free hand.

By the time the first light of day came, Pat felt she would like to help in a more practical manner.

Cautiously at first, around a corner, where Louie couldn't see them, she put the proposal to Tim.

"Why don't you let me deliver a few bottles?"

Tim looked this way and that. Then shrugged.

"Go on, then. Just take these two across to Number Forty-four. And don't forget to bring back the empties."

Happily she ran across the street with her two bottles. And she was just picking up the empties that had been left on the doorstep, when a voice like a whipcrack came out of the gray-blue sky, "So you think you got the hang of it, do yer?"

Louie. Stupid to think his beady eyes would miss a thing like this. Even with corners in the way.

He was at the end of the street, hands on hips, glower-ing through the smoke.

Pat drew herself up. She was beginning to feel mad her-self.

"Good heavens, Mr. Lay!" she said. "If you think a girl—"

"I was only checking," said Louie. "Because if you ask

me, I think it's about time you *did* start earnin' your passage." He jerked a thumb over his shoulder. "Go get yerself a handcrate. Tim—you tell her exactly what to do. Just think of her"—here the cigarette came suspiciously near to twirling—"as an extra pair of hands you been given for Christmas."

There was a jingling at another corner. It was Smitty, with a great wide smile on his face and two empties in one hand being daintily rattled together.

"Ring dem bells!" he said. "If Women's Lib hasn't scored a great big hit in—"

"Any more of that from *you*," said Louie icily, "and someone else'll score a big hit. Right on your earhole!"

Pat was delighted. At last, it seemed, she had overcome Louie's prejudices. Smitty was right. It *was* a big triumph. True, being referred to as just another pair of hands for Tim wasn't very flattering. But it was a start, and she had to admit that it would have caused too big a hold-up to have let her go off on her own with a handcrate. Some of those orders *were* terribly complicated. And in the light of day the sky *was* getting to look very stormy.

So at first she was content to act as part of the supply chain to Tim. This meant simply running back to refill one handcrate while he finished delivering from the other—by which time this second handcrate would be ready for restocking, and another cluster of empties would be ready to go back. Back and forth, back and forth. . . . There were worse jobs on cold December mornings, she guessed. At least it was keeping her warm.

But after a while, by doing this part so quickly, she found she had time to spare. So again Tim began to let her make a few deliveries herself.

"Only where the orders are straightforward, mind. Just ordinary milk orders. No extras."

"Sure, sure. Come on, then."

"All right. Those three houses at the end. Four red-tops at Twenty, two silvers at Twenty-two, three golds at Twenty-four. . . . All right?"

"All *right!*"

And away she went, glad to feel herself a true part of the system. Not so much a cog in a machine as a member of a complicated and beautiful ballet. One of the apprentice demons revolving around the Sorcerer himself. . . .

Even Louie seemed to start looking approvingly at her, after that.

Well, maybe less disapprovingly would be a better way of putting it.

But anyway, approvingly or less disapprovingly, it doesn't matter much. Because that blissful period lasted less than half an hour. It lasted until the first major calamity of the day. Or until the first major calamity came to light.

They were driving away from the second of the delivery points at which Pat had been a full working member of the team.

"How you feeling?" said Smitty.

"Great, just great!"

"That dummy training you properly?" said Smitty, with an envious glance at Tim.

"Couldn't be better," said Pat.

"And I must say, it's helping to cut down the delivery time," said Tim, ignoring Smitty's crack, and hoping to underline the value of Pat's help for Louie's benefit.

Louie said nothing. He was staring grimly ahead, pre-occupied by the thickening and massing of the clouds.

"Yeah," said Smitty, taking Tim's cue. "We're gonna be glad you came along, Pat. At this rate we might even get through *all* the deliveries before the snow comes."

Still Louie said nothing. It was the *color* of that sky as much as anything. Lead color. With yellowish tinges. Like a big bruise. One big bruise all over.

His silence was catching. This was part of the route be-tween neighborhoods—past railroad embankments and factories and vacant lots. A longer stretch of driving than usual.

Pat tried to break that silence. She was still feeling happy. She wanted *that* to be catching.

"I do love this old English custom they have," she said. "I mean the Christmas greetings that some of them leave out in their empty milk bottles."

"Greetings?" said Tim.

"Yes. Those notes you keep pulling out and reading."

Smitty laughed.

"Greetings! They're not *greetings,* love!"

"They're notes asking for extra milk," said Tim. "Or asking us to leave one bottle less. Stuff like that."

"Oh, I know!" said Pat. "But mine only had greetings on. I couldn't read them at first, but look." She pulled the scraps of paper from her pocket. "I'm saving them. Souvenirs to take back home."

That's when Louie heard.

That's when he hit the brakes.

That's when the first major calamity came to light.

Chapter Ten

Christmas Greetings to All Our Readers

Louie had nearly swallowed his cigarette.

"You—keh!" He choked. "You mean you—? Keh! Quick! Show me!"

"Well, sure," said Pat, handing him the first. "There. It's terrible writing, but when you get the hang of it it's plain enough . . . *Dear Louie, Merry Xmas.*"

"Don't you 'Dear Louie' me!" snarled Louie. "Not now. Not after this."

His hand was trembling. The scrap of paper became a blur.

"No, no!" said Pat. *"I'm* not saying it to you. That's the

message . . . *Dear Louie, Merry Xmas.* I thought it was rather sweet of—"

"Message my foot!" howled Louie. "Look!" With amazing control he managed to hold the paper still. "That's not *Dear;* that's *Please*. And that's not an *M* for *Merry;* that's a *3* for *three*. And the rest of that word is *pee-tee-ess,* short for *pints*. And *Xmas* en't *Christmas;* it's *extra*."

"Please leave 3 pints extra," murmured Tim. "But it *is* hard to make it out if you don't know."

"Who asked *you?*" growled Louie. "Now the next," he snapped to Pat. "Come on! Quick!"

"Oh, dear!" said Pat, her face as red as her parka. "But this—surely—isn't it *be of good cheer,* small *b?*"

"Nargh! That's just *it!* It en't a small *b!* It's a *6*. And *of* is *oz,* which is short for *ounces*. And that's *rum butter,* not *good cheer!*"

Pat gulped. Now that it was put like that it did seem plain enough.

"Louie," she began, "all I can say is—"

"Next!" said Louie.

She sighed and passed him the last of her "souvenirs."

"I must admit that this did seem a little premature . . . *A Happy and Prosperous New Year To You* . . . No?"

No, Pat. That last note did not say *A Happy and Prosperous New Year To You*—or to anybody else. As Louie chokingly pointed out—stabbing each word with a nicotine-stained finger that burst through a hole in his glove a little farther with every stab—that note said:

> One Large can Pineapples
> 1 jar Yoghurt
> Thank You.

Dead silence in the cab now, save for harsh nostril breathing from Louie. He was staring hard at all three notes, fanning them, turning them, holding them up to the light, even sniffing them. Pat thought he might have gone crazy with the shock. She looked at the boys. Their faces were grave. Very grave.

Smitty cleared his throat.

"Er—remember where you got them?" he asked gently.

"No. I—*oh!*" Pat gave a little yelp. "I *see!* That makes it worse, doesn't it? Oh, Louie, I am sorry, really I—"

"Quiet!"

It came as a rumble.

Louie was concentrating.

Then he slapped one of the notes down on his knee.

"Good job somebody round here can use his wits," he said ("Son of a gun!" thought Pat, "if he doesn't sound a bit *pleased!*"). "This one," said Louie, tapping the note on his knee, "it's been written on a strip torn off of a cigarette packet, right?"

"Er—yes," said Tim. "But lots of people write their notes on scraps of—"

"Yer!" growled Louie. "But look." He turned the scrap over. "See that?"

There was printing on the reverse side. The Government warning:

> These cigarettes contain substances that
> may be harmful to health.

"That'll be Mrs. Jones, Twenty-four Broughton Street. She always writes her notes on the back of that partic'lar bit. She's always on at me about smoking too much. This is her way of following up. When she's not there to lecture me in person. Women!"

Pat thought that he was being unfair again. She thought that this was really even better than wishing him a Merry Christmas, and very kind and thoughtful of Mrs. Jones. However, this was no time for pointing out such details. Pat held her tongue.

Louie was dealing with the second note. It was on pale blue paper of good quality. But the milkman was more interested in the scent.

"Yer!" he growled, after taking a deep sniff that nearly sucked it out of his hand. "Mrs. Pearson. Thirty-two Broughton Street. It's that hand cream she uses. Makes it herself. Bit too generous with the violets, I always think. Even her empty bottles smell of it."

Then he took a long look at the third note. White paper, faint ruled lines. This time it was the ink.

"Red ball-point," he murmured. "Only three people on the round use that. All teachers. And the only one we've been to so far is that Miss Spencer, Eighteen Broughton *Avenue.*"

"It figures," said Smitty, encouraged by Louie's tone. "All in the same area."

"What now, Louie?" said Tim, also encouraged.

"What *now?*" snarled Louie, revving the engine and hauling at the steering wheel as if it were someone's head he'd like to tear off. "Now we go back there and put these three orders right. What else?"

Pat felt obliged to say something. She'd apologized already, so this time she tried a little praise.

"Thank goodness you know your customers so well!"

But Louie was not to be flattered.

"Yer!" he muttered. "Marvelous, en't it? It means we've only been set back twenty minutes instead of an hour!"

He cocked an eye up at the clouds.

Pat glanced up, gulped, then pressed her lips together tight.

She'd been going to say that twenty minutes wasn't all *that* bad a delay. The skyscape changed her mind.

She'd never heard of Tubby Hooley's Golden Answer, but she was a clever girl and could work things out for herself when she set her mind to it.

And, judging from the sky, she had to admit that before long those twenty minutes might very well prove to have been vital to the whole operation.

Chapter
Eleven

The Battle
of Cooper's Hill

The second mishap was worse.

Much worse.

Much, much worse.

What made it seem such a calamity to Pat was that it wasn't even her fault, this time. But again she was the *apparent* cause of the trouble. In other words, poor Pat became patsy.

It happened (or *mis*happened) when they clashed with one of the Rely-On-Us crews.

Up until then they had simply jeered at the rival delivery-men in passing. Note that. In *passing*. Because on those occasions Rely-On-Us had either just been arriving when New Day were leaving, or vice versa.

This time it was different. This time the two crews arrived at their delivery points more or less together. Just around the corner from each other.

Well, even that might not have led to any great trouble. After all, such a coincidence was bound to happen. It happened nearly every day. The result was usually nothing worse than a little *close*-jeering, a bout or two of *in*-jeering. More personal. With custom-built quips rather than medium-range chants.

But on this particular morning there were certain extra-special factors at work.

Like one: the neighborhood.

The battlefield (for that is what it became) lay in Cooper's Hill, the neighborhood for which they'd been heading when Louie found out about the notes. As with the first delivery area, Cooper's Hill was also one of the old parts of town. It was not as poor, the houses were mostly bigger, and they had yards. But here too the streets were a warren of cul-de-sacs and squares, alleys and irregular intersections.

Yet what made it seem even more of a muddle was the "Hill" bit: the fact that it sprawled over rising ground. This had caused the original builders to scramble for choice viewpoints and easy inclines instead of planning carefully.

So—what with the steep twists and sudden turns—it was harder to service at times like these, and there was more snow lying about.

Snow. That was Number Two of the extra-special factors leading to the battle.

Pat didn't see it like that at first. She saw the extra snow left over from yesterday and looked on it as a good thing. She said so to Tim, as they began making their first deliveries around the corner from Cooper Terrace.

"That's one good thing, anyway."

"What is?"

"This snow."

"Huh?"

"Well, if it's like this with yesterday's bit of a snowfall, what will it be like when the storm comes?"

"So?"

"So we've got here before the storm, after all. A good thing."

Tim stopped. He set down his crate on the remains of a snowman, looked around, then put a hand on the girl's shoulder.

"Pat," he said, "I shouldn't mention that in front of Louie, if I were you."

"Why not? It's something to be thankful for, isn't it?"

"Yes, but wait till you see—get *lost!*"

(That last bit wasn't for Pat. It was for Roland Myers, one of the Rely-On-Us boys, who'd just bustled past with the remark, "I bet you daren't let Louie see you smooching on the job!")

"Smooching!" growled Tim, taking his hand off Pat's shoulder as if it had suddenly sprung spikes.

"Forget him," said Pat. *"Drop dead, feller!"* she called out after Roland, just to remind him whose team she was on. Then: "Now, you were saying about wait and see."

"Oh . . . yes." Tim looked worried again. "Wait till you see the second half of the round—the *route,* as you call it. That's even hillier. That's why Louie's getting all uptight, thinking about more snow up *there*."

"Oh-oh!"

"Yes. Oh-oh! Come on, let's move. We have to try and make up for that twenty minutes we lost."

A long conversation to be taking place while delivering with Louie?

Exactly. Which brings us to extra-special battle factor Number Three.

Because of the layout and general nature of Cooper's Hill, the helpers were out of Louie's sight and hearing for longer periods. For one thing, the people up there were better off than those in the first neighborhood. This meant they could afford more last-minute Christmas specials. And that meant more work for Louie.

And for another thing, with the houses being bigger and the rows shorter and the yard walls tall and thick, it meant that sounds didn't carry so easily even to Louie's sharp ears.

Remember that. Remember all those things. More snow; more cover; longer period at each point when Louie and the others were separated.

Those were the ingredients. Just as nitrogen and glycerine and cellulose are ingredients of dynamite.

All it needed next was for the New Day boys to come face to face with the Rely-On-Us boys, on foot, away from their trucks, and there you have the fuse.

And next all it needed was an excuse, and you have the spark.

And all it needed finally was for someone to apply that spark with deftness, and you have ignition and blast-off.

Pat was the excuse, the spark.

Quentin Kelly was the applier of spark to fuse.

Now Pat we know about. But Quentin Kelly is new to the scene.

New to *this* scene, anyway. New to Pat. But not new to Tim and Smitty and Louie. Oh, no! Oh dear, no! Quentin Kelly they had had trouble with before. And how![1]

For Quentin Kelly was about the nearest thing to the fallen angel Lucifer that anyone is likely to come across in modern Britain.

He was youthful—only fourteen—but you shouldn't let that fool you. He had the dark wisdom of a serpent centuries old, had Quentin Kelly.

He had an angelic appearance (so long as you didn't look too closely at his eyes, which were ice-blue with dark-red pupils)—a truly angelic appearance, with golden red hair and a fair skin.

And he had a smooth and silvery tongue. (Though here again there were some who said it was forked at the tip, if you looked closely enough.)

Well, Quentin Kelly had once used all his very considerable skill and charm to try and get a job as one of Louie's helpers. (Skill at cheating, that is. Charm at sweet-talking and flattery, we mean.) And with Louie it hadn't worked. Tim had been given the job instead.

Whereupon Kelly was so furious that the pupils of his eyes had glowed like coals and his silver tongue had flashed curses on their heads and he had sworn he would never forgive them: Tim or Louie. And time and time again he had tried to get his revenge. Now and then he had come

[1] See *Louie's SOS* for the full horrific account.

pretty close to getting it, too—only to have it blow back in his face at the last minute.

But still he persisted. Still he kept his eyes open for the slightest chance. And as a newspaper deliveryboy he was in a good position to await such chances. They didn't come often, thanks to Louie's vigilance and Tim's efficiency. But this morning . . . ah!

"Hello!" he said, cycling up on the hard-packed snow, just as Tim and Smitty and Pat were leaving the truck with a second load of deliveries. (Louie was already out of sight, measuring out a four-ounce portion of Cumberland rum butter in the kitchen of a nearby house.)

"Hello!" said Pat, thinking what a nice fresh-faced boy he looked, with his neat school blazer and school scarf and his sack of ready-folded papers.

"Just ignore him!" grunted Tim.

"Bad news!" hissed Smitty.

"I heard that," said Kelly cheerfully. "And may your turkey turn out to be as tough as old boots for such an un-charitable statement."

By now, Louie's voice could be heard, as he emerged from the house. But by now the three helpers were turning the corner, Kelly in slow, smiling pursuit.

"Don't go away," he said. "I'm only curious. I'm only wondering if business is so good that Louie's having to hire extra help."

Mild words, mildly spoken. Pat really couldn't see why Tim and Smitty should be so brusque with him.

Then Kelly himself provided the answer.

"Or is it," he said, "that you are so terribly slow? Is *that* why Louie needs extra help?"

"Get lost!" growled Tim.

"Come on," said Smitty. "Just ignore him."

But still Kelly followed. And his next remark was delivered over their heads, to the two Rely-On-Us boys who'd just turned a corner farther along.

"Hey!" sang Kelly. "Come and look at *this!* New Day's using *girls* now!"

"Heh! heh!" cackled Roland Myers. "En't they *always?*"

Now all right. Quentin Kelly didn't say it. But Roland Myers wasn't usually anything like so quick with a crack. So there must have been other forces at work. Under Kelly's influence that sort of thing was always happening.

"You say that again!" snapped Smitty, his manhood stung by this remark of Roland's. "And—*mamma mia!*—you'll wonder what hit you!"

Even Tim's non-Latin blood was roused.

"Yeah!" he growled. "You just watch it, Roly-Poly, or you'll get trundled down this hill."

Roland Myers and his friend, Pete Sharples, looked undecided. They weren't vindictive boys really. A little dumb, perhaps. But not really aggressive.

Yet under Kelly's influence . . .

"Hear what he said, Roly?" said Kelly.

"Yer! I heard him."

"He said if you'd just say that again—"

"And that's just what I'm gonna do!" said Roland, suddenly making up his mind. "I said—"

Then he frowned.

The dummy had forgotten!

"You said hasn't New Day *always* used girls," said Kelly, brightly helpful.

"Yer!" Roland nodded. "That's what I said," he went on,

glaring at Smitty. "I said—"

But that was enough for Smitty.

He had already dumped his crate on a heap of snow. Now he straightened up, swung his arm, and—flash!—he was as good as his word.

Roland *did* wonder what had hit him.

Bang on the chest, sending up a white spray.

But only for a second did he wonder.

Then, with a grunt, he was bending to make a snowball himself.

"Boys! *boys!*" pleaded Pat.

But the air was already thick with missiles.

The Battle of Cooper's Hill was on.

Chapter
Twelve

Disaster

Training tells.

The Rely-On-Us pair were still at the corner. They had all the advantage of cover, of being able to dodge out of sight whenever they wanted.

Tim and Smitty on the other hand were stuck out in the middle of the street, with nothing to hide behind but the shallow heaps of snow piled up at the edge of the sidewalk by children and householders.

But months of disciplined service with Louie made all

the difference. It gave them *system*. Synchronization. Team-work.

Very few words passed between them.

"You make," were two of them, uttered by Smitty, even as Roland and Pete were scooping up snow at the corner. "I'll fire," were the second two words, also uttered by Smitty.

"All right," said Tim, crouched down, busy already. "Just to begin with."

"Then," said Smitty, hurling a snowball at the retreating back of Roland, and scoring—*splatt!*—"I'll take a turn making."

And that was all they needed to say to switch their battle machine into action.

It worked like this:

After the first two or three snowballs, Smitty didn't have to make another during that first deadly salvo. Tim did all that, crouching, scooping, pressing, piling. And with Smitty being left to concentrate on throwing, he was able to keep up a more rapid and more accurate fire than the two Rely-On-Us boys together.

On the other hand, his throwing was almost as fast as Tim's making. There could never be any chance of Tim's making enough for them both to throw together.

Pat wondered whether to give Tim a hand, and so help make the pile big enough for both boys to throw from. But:

"No!" said Tim, when he saw her approach, crouching, ready to help. "You stay out of this, Pat. Otherwise they'll say it was three against two when we lick them."

So Pat stepped to one side, content for a while to dodge the stray snowballs and watch the System at work.

"Right!" said Smitty suddenly, as both Rely-On-Us boys dodged out of sight. "Switch places!"

Then he dropped on his knees and began scooping and pressing and piling, while Tim straightened up and took aim.

Scosh!

His first shot broke against the corner of the wall, just as Pete Sharples's nose came poking around.

And:

Spitzzz!

His second whistled over Roland's shoulder, causing that boy to throw wildly.

Smitty had already made five more snowballs—rather small, but firm and well-rounded.

"High trajectory!" he sang. "Keep 'em pinned down, Tim, and I'll be able to make enough for us both. Then we'll charge."

But alas! Smitty's strategic planning came to nothing.

Not because the Rely-On-Us boys outmaneuvered them or anything.

No.

But this two-against-two business only works when (a) the four combatants are honorable, and (b) when any bystanders present respect that honor.

Well, Tim, Smitty, Roland, and Pete were all honorable enough.

And Pat—though she was itching to join in—respected that honor.

But there was also another bystander.

There was also Kelly.

And Kelly was a respecter of nothing and nobody. No,

Disaster

sir. Especially when he saw yet another of his schemes going wrong and Tim and Smitty getting the better of the battle he had so craftily engineered.

He decided to weigh in himself. He decided to do something to distract Tim and Smitty's attention and so give that fool Rely-On-Us pair a better chance. And, being Kelly, he decided to do it with the least danger to himself—to pick on what he considered to be the weakest link—pounce and dart away.

The weakest link, in his view, was the girl.

Very carefully then, he scooped up a huge snowball of his own, secure in the knowledge that the boys were too busy making and firing their own snowballs, and that Pat was too busy watching them, to notice him.

Then—scrunch! scrunch!—quite softly—he hurried forward: one hand poised with the snowball, the other hand ready to snatch back Pat's parka hood. Again, being Kelly, he wasn't going to risk wasting that missile. He was going to stuff it right down the back of that girl's neck.

Now . . . All right . . .

All very cunning. All very well, if wickedly, thought out.

But what Kelly didn't know, of course, was what Tim had learned the hard way the evening before. That malevolent machinating scheming serpent of a boy didn't know about that slightly built girl's expensive training, back in the gym at Ward Ridge.

Pat heard those stealthy scrunching footsteps. At the very last moment she heard them. And this time it was *her* training that paid dividends.

Instead of swerving around like any untrained girl, she stayed put. She stayed exactly put, save that she suddenly sent messages to certain back and shoulder and arm muscles.

Poor Kelly!

Snowball or knife, he didn't know it was all the same to a judo expert when she hears stealthy footsteps coming up behind her like that.

And Pat was an Orange Belt (under-16 group).

Kelly took the last fateful step. He lifted the snowball. He reached out to the parka. He even got a fingerhold on the peak of the hood.

Then Pat reacted.

She stooped slightly. Her left arm came back. Kelly felt as if invisible hooks had suddenly caught his sleeve. Then one of Pat's legs came back, neatly, gracefully, and Kelly felt as if the fairies had put little silver wheels under his shoes.

And then Kelly flew, just as Tim had flown the evening before, but faster. He flew faster than Tim because Pat had decided he should, not out of spite, but simply because she had aimed him at a softer landing strip—the low bank of piled-up snow at the edge of the sidewalk.

"Yeeeeh!"

Kelly's scream was chilling to hear, even in that already chill air.

The combatants on both sides stopped in mid-aim or mid-scoop or mid-retreat and stared.

Then Kelly landed. A perfect three-point, just as Pat had planned it: both shoulders and backside.

But . . .

There was one thing she hadn't planned on.

She may have been an Orange Belt at physical judo.

Sure.

But Quentin Kelly was a Black Belt (all-age group) at mental karate. Or he would have been if that sport had ever been officially recognized.

Quick as a cobra.

Dirty as a double-agent.

Deadly.

That was Kelly when his cunning came into play.

So although he fell nice and softly (uncomfortably, mind, and foolishly) slap where Pat had intended, he was stung into furious retaliation.

Mental retaliation—against which there are no known judo holds.

"What is this at the side of me, on the snow bank?" his diabolically quick brain said, in one milli-flash.

"It is that Tim fool's handcrate, loaded with gold-top milk and special double creams," came the reply, in the next milli-flash.

"So why not lash out with your feet?" was the question his brain popped in the third milli-flash. "All accidental-like?"

"Why not indeed, and so get Louie mad at them?" was the response.

All in four small fractions of a flash, even at the moment of impact.

Then he put it into operation.

Out lashed his legs. Over crashed the crate.

"What the—*what's going on here?*" came the howl from a corner.

Kelly opened his left eye, saw Louie, suppressed a smirk, pretended not to have heard, and howled himself, *"Now look what you made me do!"*

There was no getting away from it. There was the up-turned crate, with cream and rich Channel Island milk oozing onto the snow, and there was Kelly, flat on his back beside it. *He* wasn't to blame, his expression said. *He* had just been flung there.

The Rely-On-Us boys melted, vanished.

The snowballs in Tim and Smitty's hands began to do the same.

"Oh, gosh!" said Pat. "I—I just don't know—"

But Louie did.

He took one look at the face of the boy on his back on the snow and Louie knew exactly what had happened.

For once his glare wasn't directed at Pat or either of his boys. They'd be getting it later, the flickering glint in his eyes said, but right now—

"Up!" he said, sticking out the point of his boot, ready to stir Kelly into life.

Well, quality tells as well as training. And Kelly certainly had quality. Seeing his move was beginning to misfire, he pulled another one.

"Yes, sir," he groaned, humbly, willingly—beginning to sit up. "I—*oooOW!!"*

The cry arrested even Louie.

"Eh?"

"OoooOW!" cried Kelly, suddenly flopping back, hands clawing desperately at his left leg. "My—*oooOW!*—my—my leg. I—I think I—I think she broke it!"

"Oh, gosh!" gasped Pat, darting forward. "Oh, dear! Oh, I—I *am* sorry!"

"Lucky for you if she did!" growled Louie, glaring

down at Kelly. "Because I was just about to break your neck!"

It was an unfeeling thing to say. But he *knew* Quentin Kelly, remember.

Even so, there was a doubt in his voice as he said it. Kelly *might* have been lying. Kelly *might* have been telling the truth as he felt it—crying before he was hurt. Or Kelly *might* have been telling the truth, period.

Louie just couldn't afford to take chances, and Kelly knew it.

"*OoooOW!*" he groaned again.

"Honestly, I am sorry!" said Pat.

Kelly looked up at her. He gave a marvelous performance then. He managed to bring to his face what looked like a brave smile.

"That—that's O.K. You—ouch!—you couldn't know. I forgive you."

Smitty looked as if he could have thrown up. He too knew Kelly.

Tim wasn't so sure. Kelly's performance was superb and Tim was a more trusting boy than Smitty.

Pat now had two fat frank tears glistening on her cheeks.

Then Louie growled, "Well, go on then, one of yer! You, Smitty. Phone for an ambulance."

It was all they could do. If the boy's leg wasn't broken and they'd been fooled, another twenty precious minutes would be wasted, at least. But if it was broken, to have left him lying there in the snow, at *Christmas,* would have blackened their names forever.

Kelly had them on toast and he knew it.

So did Louie.

Cold toast, but toast.

When Pat said, "Here, take my parka to lie on!" Louie stopped her.

"No," he said.

"Why not?" said Pat.

"Yes—ouch!—why not?" said Kelly. "My back's getting wet."

"Because the slightest movement might disturb the fracture," said Louie, giving his watch a savage glance. "And you wouldn't want to lose that leg, would yer?"

Kelly sighed, but said nothing. Wet back or not, it was worth it to see Louie glancing at that watch, suffering with every tick.

In fact, it was twenty-*three* minutes before the ambulance arrived. And another four minutes passed before the ambulance men pronounced the leg O.K.

Kelly didn't protest. He didn't want to waste more time than was necessary, either. He didn't fancy spending the rest of the morning being X-rayed. Besides, it would make his triumph even sweeter to rub things in a little.

"Well do you know," he said, giving the ambulance men a shy smile as he got to his feet, "even the pain's gone now!"

"Yes, well, it does sometimes happen," said the senior of the two.

"Blow me down if I don't feel fit enough to do a jig!" said Kelly, doing just that, his grin broadening.

Louie stepped forward.

"If you've been deliberately having on us—" he growled, as Kelly nimbly dodged behind the ambulance men.

"Now, now, sir!" said the senior man, shaking his head

at Louie. "You mustn't be like that. The lad was probably in shock. He—"

But Kelly was safe.

Louie had turned already. He was already crouching over the spilled bottles, telling his helpers to get a move on.

For now the sky seemed suddenly to have burst. Huge flakes were coming down, floating, bobbing, spiralling, whirling, settling.

The storm had broken and the New Day team had not even completed the first half of the route.

Chapter Thirteen

The Second Battle of Cooper's Hill

This next battle was much more punishing.

The first battle of Cooper's Hill had been fun while it lasted. No matter which way it seemed likely to swing, the warriors on either side had felt throughout that it was all worth-while. The worst that could happen was— Well, it had in fact *happened*. Milk had been spilled. Cream also. Louie had intervened. Bad, bad, and very bad. But it did not mean the end of the world. They had *survived,* hadn't they?

But this next battle was different. The worst that could

happen this time was— Well, they didn't like to think about it. And there were moments when it did really look like the end of the world. The Flood all over again, but in crystallized form. Moments in which they felt lost to all mankind, cut off, obliterated.

Because this next battle wasn't with any human being, even one as maliciously mischievous as Quentin Kelly, or as furiously formidable as Louie. This next battle was with a snowstorm a million times as malicious as Kelly at his most mischievous (which is saying a lot) and about thirty-five times as formidable as Louie at his most furious (which is saying quite a lot more).

Obliterated. Obliterating. Whichever way you shake it, that's the word. Flakes that clung together seemed to be coming down as snowballs themselves, ready-made, but lighter so that they floated, and with ordinary flakes fluttering in the spaces between them, forming filmy curtains— curtain beyond curtain between your eyes and the nearest other person or object. And, since they settled thickly the instant they stopped floating or swirling or fluttering, the chances were that that other object or person had such a thick coating of white that you missed him, her, or it until you collided.

Luckily, Louie—

No. Correction. Luck rarely entered into it where Louie was concerned. Prudently, then . . .

Prudently, Louie had already put the chains on the truck wheels before starting out that morning. And prudently, he had decided to bring a shovel along. Those two precautions helped get them out of the corner (exposed, steeper than usual, out of the way) that they found themselves in when the storm first broke.

But it was something he didn't dare to risk twice.

"Sorry," he said—or at least that's what it sounded like, for he said it as soon as he got out of the cab at the next point, and the snow was obliterating sounds as well as sights, was even engulfing and extinguishing his cigarette—"but from now on . . ."

"What?" yelled Smitty. *"Whassat?"*

"FROM NOW ON . . . WE STICK . . . TO THE . . . MAIN STREETS."

"Main*stream?*"

"Main *streets,* ya dupple!"

Well, it sounded like "dupple." But just then one of the larger clusters of flakes had clapped itself against Louie's mouth and nose like a gag, and the word was probably "dummy."

Anyway, that's beside the point. And what *was* the point soon became clear enough, even if nothing else in that blizzard was.

Sticking to the main streets meant a better chance of getting the truck rolling again, yes. But it also meant longer journeys on foot and with handcrate. In all *that* stuff.

Pat remembered reading a book called *The Worst Journey in the World.* That was about snow, too. Up in the Arctic somewhere. Now she could understand it better—the use of the word "worst"—as she stuck close to Tim and the snow stuck closer still to them both.

"Good heavens above!" a customer would sometimes say, peeping out of a crack in the door. "I never thought you'd be out in *this!*"

Or—from some comedian, "Hey! Look! Louie's trained *snowmen* for the job!"

Or—from some sympathetic soul, "Come inside! Come

inside and shelter till it stops!"

Stops! As if it ever would stop, from the looks of it!

But then, even as Pat was thinking this, there came the first lull. The blizzard abated to just a normal heavy snowfall. The clusters thinned out, or held back, or regrouped, somewhere above, and through the ordinary flakes objects and people became visible at all of ten feet again.

That was welcome, of course, but not very cheering.

It showed too well how much damage the snow was doing. Already, in only a half hour, there must have been another two inches to add to yesterday's layer. And in places it was drifting.

"Drifting!" said Tim, shaking a miniature snowstorm from his head and shoulders. "That's just the worst possibub . . ."

He'd meant to say "possible." He'd meant to say, "That's just the worst possible thing it could do." But the big stuff was falling again and one of the leading clusters had swirled into his mouth.

It was just after that that Pat got lost.

Several times it had nearly happened. This time, when a long howling gust of wind started causing it to snow upward as well as down, it really did happen.

She had just crossed the street and, tottering on platform soles of caked ice, made her deliveries, when Tim, and the opposite side of the street itself, and even some of the houses on her own side, vanished.

Coming from where she did, she thought of tornadoes.

"Tim!" she wailed. "Tib! Shim!" (The big clusters were coming thick and fast now.) "Ti-im!" she cried, cupping her hands around her mouth.

No answer.

She tottered and clumped and slid to the other side.

Still no Tim.

Only two of the bottles he'd just delivered. Outside a door. Already half obliterated, their silver tops hazed over in a blank stare.

"Oh, *Tim!*" she cried, this time without any distortion, because it was really more of a sob of despair, directed with a bowed head onto the front of her parka.

She came very close to panic then.

What should she *do?* she wondered.

Stay put?

Knock on a door and ask to shelter?

Try to find her way back to the truck?

The first was unthinkable. The second was also unthinkable, when she imagined the hold-up it would cause the others, the time wasted in searching for her. Her! She who had caused such a dreadful waste of time already!

She picked up her crate and walked, bent in half against the wind, feeling her cheeks go numb.

She intended to turn the corner around which she and Tim had first arrived, but what with the wind and the numbness and being bent like that, she missed it.

Must have.

Because when she straightened up, out of the worst of the wind, and looked around, she found herself in a dead-end, in a street that simply couldn't be the one leading back to the truck.

"Tim! Tooeeb! Tum! Tcha! . . . Ti-im!"

It was eerie.

Another lull, very brief, showed her that the houses here

weren't even inhabited. Peering through the dancing flakes, the lighter flakes, she saw a sight that put her in no mood for joining any dance. She saw death and desolation: the corpse of a street, with boards nailed across its many eyes.

"Tim!" she cried, nearly screaming it. "Ti—!"

And then she did scream, as a hand clutched her shoulder.

It says a lot for how panicky she had become that it never even crossed her mind to counter with a judo hold. Orange Belt or not, at Ward Ridge she had received her lessons in a nice warm airy brightly lit gym, not a raging blizzard.

And maybe it was as well.

In fact, *absolutely certainly* it was as well.

After all, it would never have done for her to send Louie into orbit the way she had despatched Tim and Quentin Kelly.

" 'Smarrer with yer?!"

His voice was slightly muffled but clear enough. Louie had already conquered the snow-cluster-in-the-mouth problem by masking the bottom half of his face with a large handkerchief. The trouble was that he'd refined that solution by tearing a hole in it just big enough to insert his cigarette, and the sight of that dead-white face with the glowing hole nearly caused Pat to faint on the spot.

"C'm on!" said Louie, in a voice that was reasonably gentle, considering what he was going through—a voice like a file, sure enough, but a file being drawn across wood instead of metal. "You're safe now. Take more 'n this to get *me* lost!"

Chapter
Fourteen

A Christmas-card
View—Or a
Glimpse of Hell?

The battle against the blizzard lasted three hours alto-
gether, and for the last two of them Pat had a headquarters
view of it.

After the incident in which she nearly got lost, the girl
was switched from delivering to assisting at the truck itself.

She didn't mind. It made sense. It was no easy task, and
she was able to make herself much more useful: helping
Louie and the boys to reload the handcrates, restacking the
empties, and seeing that the snow didn't pile too thickly on
the truck.

That last chore in particular was useful. The snow was

coming down so heavily, and Louie and the boys were having to make such long sorties, that it could easily have obliterated the contents of the truck in the intervals, if Pat hadn't been busy all the time, brushing it off as it landed. In fact, it soon became apparent that this chore was more than useful. It was vital. Struggling through the snow was difficult enough, but if at the end of every sortie the boys and the man had had to embark on a further struggle just to find the items they required next, they would surely have had to give in.

But they didn't give in. Almost everyone else did, but not New Day Dairies.

Once, when Louie ran out of cigarettes (three pulls each was about the most he could manage before the snow got to it, making it too soggy to keep alight), he sent Pat to a corner store within sight of the truck for another pack. It was one of those tiny stores that are very common in older parts of British towns, selling anything from hair oil to darning needles, candles to candies.

"But I didn't know you'd started selling newspapers," said a customer in front of Pat, pointing to a damp-looking pile on the counter.

"Nor have I," said the woman behind the counter. "I'm just holding these as a favor. The paper boy—that nice-mannered lad with the red hair—he said it was just too bad out there to deliver another single one. He said would I mind having them here, and giving them out to any of his customers who happened to come in later. Well, can you blame the lad? In *this?*"

Even though Pat had a strong suspicion who that "nice-mannered lad" was, she too had to agree. Who *could* blame him for abandoning his route in a storm like that?

All the same, it was with a glow of pride that she ordered the cigarettes, and said who they were for, and let the women know that New Day Dairies had not abandoned *their* customers.

And when—during a lull about half an hour later—their truck went lurching and rattling past a lunch counter, her pride glowed brighter. For there, parked outside, little more than a huge mound of snow itself, was the Rely-On-Us truck. And there, wiping a clear space with his sleeve in the steamed-up window of the lunch counter, was the Rely-On-Us deliveryman, blinking out into the snow at the passing truck as if he couldn't believe his eyes.

"See that?" said Louie.

"Yer!" said Smitty. "Chickensville."

"They'll be dumping next," said Tim.

"True enough," said Louie.

"Dumping?" said Pat.

"Yer!" said Smitty. "Dumping their deliveries at street corners."

"Strategic points," said Tim.

"Stacks of crates," said Louie. "For their customers to come and get their own."

"But—how do they know their customers will realize what to do?" asked Pat.

"Oh, Rely-On-Us customers always know what to do," said Smitty. "Ten flakes of snow in any one half hour and it's put your coat and hat on and go and fetch it yourself."

"Yes, but—don't some people take more than they need? Don't people who're not customers just help themselves? And what about *new* customers? Those who don't know the routine when it snows?"

"They get to know what tea without milk tastes like," said Tim.

"Cut the talking," said Louie. "It's coming on heavy again. We still might have to do a bit of dumping ourselves."

But they knew he didn't mean it. They knew he would have spent the rest of the year, all seven days of it, crawling from house to house—bottle by bottle, egg by egg, portion of rum butter by portion of rum butter—sooner than let down any of *his* customers. They knew too that he would have had all three of *them* doing it along with him. And still they felt such a glow of pride—Tim and Smitty as well as Pat—that it was a wonder the snow wasn't melted right there and then within a radius of twenty feet.

Yes. Three hours. That was the duration of the second battle of Cooper's Hill. At the end of it there was over a foot of snow on the ground and, in many places, because of the drifting, much more than that.

But also at the end of it Louie and his three helpers had completed the first half of the route. No one had been left without milk, or cream, or eggs, or canned peaches, or Cumberland rum butter, or anything else they had ordered.

"Wow!" said Smitty, finally sitting down in the cab with a thud. "Mission accomplished."

"Yes," said Tim. "Wow!"

"I second that," said Pat.

"Correction," said Louie.

They looked at him.

"Correction?" asked Smitty.

"Yer!" grunted Louie. *"Half* a mission accomplished.

Soon's we've had a break an' a bite to eat, we've got *that* lot to see to."

He nodded, indicating the view in front of them.

It was a beautiful view. A perfect living Christmas-card view.

The sky was clearing rapidly. The dull yellow-tinged gray was giving place to a light powdery blue, through which the sun was shining again. And even as they watched, the powderiness itself was clearing, the blue deepening, and the sun brightening.

Then they had to squint as it sparkled and shone and flashed on the fresh snow: on the road in front of them; on the roofs of the factories below them (for they were still on the side of Cooper's Hill); on the banks of the pewter-gray river winding beyond the factories; and on the hillside rising beyond that—a steeper, broader hillside than the one they were on now.

"Wailey Heights!" sighed Smitty.

"Yes," murmured Tim.

Pat mistook their quietness for awe in the face of so much beauty. For this Wailey Heights was like fairyland under that fresh covering of snow. Even an ordinary hillside would have looked good just then, glittering in the sun—even a bare hillside of fields. And if it had been broken up with trees—dark tall pines, say—it would have looked better still.

But Wailey Heights was covered with houses as well as trees. And this time the builders had planned wisely. The streets and avenues had been looped around that hillside like ornaments on a Christmas tree—gracefully, decoratively—with an eye to natural contours, dips, hollows, spurs, escarpments.

Maybe on any ordinary day this wouldn't have been quite so apparent. Maybe only at night, with windows lit and street lights on, would the patterns have normally emerged. But now, in the snow, with the roofs and blacktop surfaces of the roads obliterated, it was the warm red-brick sides of the houses that stood out, and the sun-reflecting windows, and the blue smoke spiralling from the chimneys. This was better than just any old landscape under snow, thought Pat. This was a true Christmas landscape, with a promise of firesides and parties, Santa Claus and bulky presents at the foot of a thousand beds.

"Five hundred houses to deliver at," said Smitty, with another sigh.

"Over a thousand bottles of milk," said Tim.

"Well over," said Louie. "And that's without the extras."

No. It hadn't been the beauty of the scene that had subdued those three. Pat might have seen a Christmas-card view; but they had caught a glimpse of Hell.

"Let's just hope there'll be no more snow," said Smitty.

"Even if there isn't," said Louie, "it'll be no picnic up Wailey Heights. When you can't see Wailey Pond you know it's bad already."

He had been making entries in the thick order book—checking no doubt to see that nothing had been overlooked back on the first half of the route. Now he snapped it shut.

"It could take us all afternoon and well into the evening," he said.

"Well I don't mind," said Pat.

"Nor me," said Tim.

"Me neither," said Smitty. "Only—" He turned to Louie with a frown. "I've been thinking, Louie. Like you say, we'll have our work cut out with Wailey Heights, won't we?"

Louie started the engine.

"Yer. So?"

"So—well—we won't be bothering with Hardcastle Grange, will we?"

Pat felt a thrill of extra pleasure at the sound of that name.

"Hardcastle Grange?" she said. "It sounds like one of those big old English mansions you read about in detective stories. Is it?"

"Yeah!" said Smitty. "I don't know about detectives, but that's what it is, all right. About two miles out in the country. Beyond Wailey Heights. You can just see the top of Hardcastle Hill in the distance." He turned back to Louie. "It'll be murder out there in this! Those country roads."

"So?" said Louie again, his cheekbones beginning to shine.

Smitty ignored the sign.

"So—well—hey, come *on,* Louie! We've no other customers out that way. And there's only the gardener and his wife left. All the others at the Grange have gone on holiday. We can't go all that way . . . in this . . . just for . . ."

Smitty tailed off.

He'd noticed the cheekbones at last. And the eyes. And the intensity of the glow of the cigarette under the eyes.

"For one thing," said Louie, "when I take an order"—he seemed about to choke—"that's it. I mean to deliver. For another thing"—he began to scratch his arm—"that woman. Gardener's wife. She's not been too well lately."

Pat felt another thrill. It looked as if they would be visiting that real old English mansion after all.

"Gee, Mr. Lay!" she said, hoping to encourage him in his determination (as if Louie needed it!). "That is one very kind thought!"

Louie looked as if he could spit.

"Kind nothin'!" he said. "It's just that I'd never hear the end of it if I let her down."

Tim explained to Pat, "She used to get her milk from Rely-On-Us, you see. Till *they* let her down."

"Yer!" grunted Louie. "So you can imagine what that bunch of creeps would say if we did the same." The truck began to move. "Now let's get back to the dairy. Then you easy-livers can go get something to eat while I assemble the heavy snow gear. Get *plenty* to eat. It might be your last meal before your Christmas dinners." He glanced at the sky. "Only don't take too long. I want you all back by one o'clock sharp."

It was twelve already. It would probably take them half an hour to get back to the dairy in the fresh snow.

But no one complained. They had all seen what Louie had seen.

More ragged yellow-gray clouds. With bruise-purple outriders scudding before them.

Chapter Fifteen

Pat's Great Idea

At one o'clock sharp, Tim and Smitty returned to the dairy.

Considering they'd had only thirty minutes to get home and back, and had had to change their socks and pants and dry themselves out generally, and had had to convince their mothers that they couldn't quit now, that a boy's got to do what a boy's got to do (if he's one of Louie's boys, that is) —considering all these things, it hadn't left them much time to "get *plenty* to eat." It hardly left them time to get anything to eat, in fact.

That is why Smitty had taken the precaution of stuffing his pockets with chestnuts again—this time ready roasted, peeled, and salted. And that is why Tim was still munching a ham sandwich, with another four packed safely away in his pockets.

"Still guzzlin'?"

That was Louie's greeting.

"Still guzzlin'?"

That, if you please, was all he had to say to them, when they arrived, dead on time. After a mere half-hour break, remember. After all they'd been through on his behalf that morning.

"Anyone else said that," Tim confided to Smitty later, "and I'd have turned right round and gone home and watched the telly."

"Me, too," Smitty had replied. "Only before I turned right round I'd have pelted him with chestnuts. Good and hard. *Mamma mia!* Did you ever know such a guy? Sometimes I wonder . . ."

But of course anyone else but Louie would have spent some of that half hour having a snack himself, and Louie obviously had not. Louie had obviously been too busy, not only checking that the truck was loaded with all the milk and specials required for the second half of the route, but also with the "heavy snow gear" he'd mentioned.

This in itself must have taken up a good ten minutes of that half hour, since it included:

> 2 extra shovels
> 2 extra-heavy-duty yard brushes
> 4 large sacks filled with a sand-and-salt mixture
> 1 large sack filled with coal cinders
> 2 short but stout planks
> 1 blowtorch.

And not only had these items to be found and assembled, they'd also had to have places found for them on the already tightly packed vehicle.

"Did *you* get anything to eat?" asked Tim, reaching for his spare sandwiches. His indignation had suddenly curdled into a feeling of guilt.

"Yer. Canna peaches."

"Peaches?"

Tim shivered at the thought. Smitty rolled his eyes.

"Fastest food there is," said Louie. "Very nourishing."

"Fu-fastest?"

Louie nodded.

"You can drink 'em straight out of the can. Bein' slippery they don't need chewing. Like oysters. You want to try it sometime. . . . Well"—his eyes went beady as he looked at his watch—"two minutes past. Looks like our passenger's had enough."

The boys looked around.

No sign of Pat.

For some reason Tim felt disappointed—almost let down.

"Maybe—maybe she got held up," he said. "Being a guest, she can't just march in and tell them to look quick with the food."

Louie was shaking his head.

"Nergh! She's just had enough. Packed in for the day. These jet-setters are all alike. I knew all along we wouldn't be seeing *her* again today. Anyway, time we was moving. It's—"

He stopped.

Stared.

His jaw didn't drop *exactly*. But his cigarette drooped

until the end nearly scorched his chin.

Pat was just turning into the yard.

She looked very chipper in a different parka—more of an orange-red this time—and light blue ski pants.

But it wasn't her clothes that Louie and the boys were gaping at. It was what she was dragging across the yard behind her.

A train of three sleds. Kids' sleds, medium size, two rather battered and one brand new.

"Hi! Sorry I'm late but—"

"What d'you think you're *on?*" growled Louie. "Winter sports? Think this is Saint Moritz? Eh? That it?"

He was nearly choking again at the sight of such frivolous objects at a time like this.

"Oh, *these?*" said Pat, smiling broadly, proudly. "Well that's why I'm late. I've had to go around the Peters' neighbors rustling them up. Borrowing them from the kids. It took some doing because of course they were hoping to use them themselves. But I managed to bribe them with candy and promise to pay for any damage. It was almost like renting a car, the way some of them—"

"Never mind all *that!* We got a job to do. Remember? Huh? Hah? Now if you want to help, help. If you want to play, play. But—"

"But this *is* helping. Don't you see? If we can't get into all the side streets up Wailey Heights, why these will be just the thing for the extra hand loads. It'll save—"

"Um," said Louie. "Yer. Well."

"That's a *terrific* idea, Pat!" cried Tim, translating Louie's three grunts into plain English.

"*Benissimo!*" sang Smitty. "Here, have a few chestnuts.

What gave you that idea?"

"Oh, it's not mine really," said Pat. "Up in New England, where they get snow like this for weeks and weeks—and where they *still* deliver milk, *and* in bottles"—she flashed at Louie—"they find sleds very useful in these conditions."

But Louie had recovered by now.

"Not if they stand yakking about in the dairy yards, they don't!" he said. "So come on. Drag 'em over to the van and let's see where we can fit them in."

Chapter
Sixteen

Louie
Attacked

Pat found the second half of the route much different from the first. The houses on Wailey Heights were modern, with brighter paintwork and better designs—more like a model city back home—but it wasn't just that. Mainly it was the people.

Not that there was anything greatly different about the people in Cooper's Hill or the neighborhood before that. It was simply the fact that there were more of them around in the afternoon.

On the first part of the morning half of the route there had been few people around because of the earliness of the hour.

And on the second part of the morning half of the route there had been few people around because of the blizzard.

But that Christmas Eve afternoon the whole of Wailey Heights seemed to be swarming with men, women, and children. Especially children.

This was a holiday for most of them, Pat remembered. And the snow had held off. The sky had become thickly overcast. The sun was no more than a fuzzy lemon hole in the clouds from time to time. So it was left to the snow that had already fallen to brighten the scene. That, and the people who'd swarmed out to work in it and to play in it.

"You can see Wailey Pond all right *now*," said Smitty, as the truck approached it, its chains and bottles clinking and jingling like reindeer harness; like sleigh bells.

Even Pat didn't have to ask where to look.

The pond lay at the foot of Wailey Heights, just beyond the river, at the other side of the bridge they would soon be crossing. And the reason it could be spotted so easily was because it had been swept clean, making a dark smooth oval in the surrounding whiteness—a dark smooth oval alive with colors. Blues, reds, yellows, greens. Sliding, slithering, mingling, breaking, as in a kaleidoscope. The colors of the sweaters and hats and flying scarves and flashing socks of the people skating there.

Or trying to.

"Ouch!" gasped Tim, as they rattled past the pond. "It's a good thing that fat kid's well padded!"

"Just think of the roast chestnuts we could sell there," murmured Smitty, deep in thoughts of his own.

"At Ward Ridge they teach us figure-skating as part of

the winter-sport course," said Pat.

Louie blew ash off his cigarette. Not exactly a snort. But, "Seem to teach you some funny stuff at that place," he grunted.

"Oh, well," said Pat, "you never know when it might come in useful."

"Yer!" Louie sniffed. "That judo this morning. That was *very* useful, wasn't it?"

Pat was about to protest, but Tim gave her a nudge and Smitty gave her a quick shake of the head. So she just shrugged her shoulders and let it go.

Anyway, there was no more time for arguing. As the boys could have told her, Louie was very skilled at getting in the last word just as he was bringing the truck to a stop. It was the same now. They were among the houses, at the first delivery point.

From then on they were busy. But because it wasn't a battling busy-ness—with whirling snow blinding them and blocking their ears and obliterating their words—it was enjoyable. And, as Pat had guessed, her sleds came in useful right away. The main feeder roads of Wailey Heights— the bus routes—had been plowed already. No problem there. But many of the side roads were still deep in snow and would have been tricky to negotiate.

"Good thing you thought about *these,* Pat," said Tim, in a loud voice for Louie's benefit, as they lifted the sleds off the truck.

"Yes," said Smitty, also overly-loud, "if you hadn't thought of these, we'd soon have been forced to use sand and salt and shovels and all that other junk."

"All right!" snapped Louie. "You made yer point. And it

still might come to shovels yet, so get movin' while you can."

Smitty winked at Pat. Tim gave her the thumbs-up sign.

It wasn't often that a helper scored off Louie.

And rarer still that Louie conceded the point.

So that was the first thing that cheered her up.

The second was the people themselves. The kids were playing everywhere—some with sleds of their own, some having snowfights, some building snowmen, some attempting to construct igloos (very serious, these were), and some rolling huge snowballs (with giggles and gleeful grunts at the idea of making them big enough to bowl over a bus). The fathers were mainly in their own front paths and driveways—digging, scraping, chipping away—and grunting . . . and puffing . . . and making it an excuse to stop and have a few words of chat whenever the deliverers arrived with the milk.

The mothers were mostly inside, but nearly everywhere they would come to the door, relieved to hear the clinking of the bottles and to know that the morning's blizzard hadn't endangered their supplies. Often their faces would be flushed from bending over the stove, and as they opened the door they would let out delicious smells of baking: freshly cooked mince pies, sausage rolls . . .

Pat came to know British sausage rolls that afternoon. Like hot dogs but encased in warm crisp pastry instead of bread. And Tim and Smitty renewed their acquaintance with that dish over and over again.

Smitty had no need of his chestnuts.

Tim could have left his sandwiches at home.

At house after house, the New Day delivery crew were

offered (and they accepted) mince pies or slices of Christmas cake, sausage rolls or crisp cheese straws, cups of milky coffee or nips of something stronger.

The helpers gorged themselves on pies, cake, rolls, straws, and milky coffee in that first hour. But Louie refused all nips of something stronger, even of his own elderberry wine.

"It 'ud be bad enough being drunk in charge of a milk van any time. But on a day when there might be another blizzard—no thanks!"

He accepted cigars and packs of cigarettes, though. The Christmas spirit was getting to him. There was even an incident in which—well—you couldn't exactly say he let his hair down. But . . .

"Let's roll it on Louie!" cried a boy of about ten, leader of one of the snowball-rolling gangs.

It was a huge missile by then, just ripe for launching. Bigger than all five kids who'd been working on it, it was poised just right, up a short steep side-track that branched off at the side of the truck.

Louie was by himself. The others weren't far away, though, just around the corner, on their way back, dragging their sleds.

"Hey! Stay back! Just watch this!" said Smitty. "Let's see how he handles it."

Louie was going on with his restacking, getting the truck ready for the next delivery point.

"You roll that on *me*," he growled, not even looking around, "and you'll eat yer Christmas dinners in the hospital. Fancy that, do yer?"

Some of the gang looked uneasy.

But the leader plucked up courage.

"Gern!" he ventured.

("That's a bold lad!" whispered Tim. "Must be high on chocolate liqueurs," agreed Smitty.)

"You heard me!" came Louie's growl, between the clashes of the crates he was manhandling. "Shove off!"

The gang looked at one another. The leader's grin wobbled.

But he *was* a bold lad.

Louie's growl may have deterred him from using the ultimate weapon, but he wasn't going to lose face with his followers.

"All right," he said, stooping and snatching up an ordinary snowball. "Well, take *that* then!"

And Louie took it. Back of the neck.

He froze.

("He can't believe it!" gasped Smitty gleefully. "It's struck him paralytic!")

Louie's immobility must have encouraged the other kids.

"Yer!" another of them cried. "Let's snowball Louie!"

And they all began to stoop and scoop.

Then Louie moved.

"Rrrright!" he roared.

And it was as if the morning's blizzard had returned, all dressed up in a blue sweater and with a flaring cigarette in its mouth.

Pat gaped.

Smitty and Tim together had been something out of this world in their snowballing tactics during the first battle of Cooper's Hill. But Louie alone was out of this universe.

Fizz!

Splatt!

Whizz!

Blatt!

This was the master. The boss. This just had to be the greatest snowball-fighter of all time.

Quick—so quick you couldn't even see him making them. He stooped and the snowballs were just *there,* one at each fingertip.

And accurate—every one of them found a target.

And humane—none was too hard-packed, and the targets were never faces but chests, backs, hands drawn back with snowballs of their own, and mid-air snowballs coming his way.

"Computerized!" gasped Tim.

"Ground-to-air!" murmured Smitty.

"And very effective," said Pat.

The kids had begun by squealing with delight to have stung Louie into action. But now they were fleeing.

Tim, Smitty, and Pat turned the corner and approached the truck. On Smitty's advice, they pretended not to have noticed the incident.

Louie, for his part, pretended he'd been doing nothing but sorting the empties and rearranging the load.

"Where you lot been?" he snapped. "Foolin' around? This is a milk-delivery job, not a ski-party!"

After that, Pat's spirits became more buoyant than ever.

She began to notice the trees—the Christmas trees in the windows of the houses—their multicolored lights beginning to glow and twinkle, their tinsel to glitter more sharply. And she began to notice the sounds, too—some of them as full of Christmas promise as those lights and garlands. From radios and television sets came the strains of Christmas music: television commercials with jingles as light and airy as the tinsel on the trees, radio programs reverberating and resounding with ancient carols sung in medieval chapels by young choirs.

Even the scraping of shovels seemed to take on a Christmas ring, harmonizing with the shrill cries of the snow-happy children and the harsh voices of adults, rasping Christmas greetings, exchanging wisecracks.

One particular exchange involved Louie and a mailman.

"Hey up!" Smitty whispered. "Here comes Bob!"

"Bob?"

"Yes. Him with the sack on his back. Used to go to school with Louie."

"This you mustn't miss," said Tim. "Sparks always fly when these two meet."

"He's got a tongue nearly as sharp as Louie's. . . . Here we go. Seconds out. Round One."

Bob was shorter than Louie, but broader. His face was red and there was a sprig of mistletoe in his cap. He, too, had a cigarette that looked like a permanent fixture in his mouth, and his eyes had the same beady glitter as Louie's.

The mailman led with a verbal straight left.

"You think *you* got a tough job, Lou, mate—but how about us?"

Louie countered, circling cautiously, "Where was *you* in the blizzard 's morning, then?"

Bob rode that punch, backing a little.

"I was busy tryin' to read the addresses on some of

these envelopes."

Quick as a flash, Louie pounced.

"Ha!" It was a bark of triumph. "Hear that? Hear what he just said?" His hand swept down and back and into his pants pocket. When it emerged it was holding a sheaf of paper scraps. "How about some of the writing *we've* got to read?"

Pat's cheerfulness ebbed a little as she recognized her "souvenirs."

"Give 'em here!" said Bob.

His eyes went beadier as he squinted at the first note.

"Well, it's easy," he said. "Nothing to it. This one says *Louie for King!* . . . And this one says *Please do not disturb* . . . And this is—why!—it's a pome! It says:

> Hush, hush, whisper who dares?
> Louie the milkman is watering his wares."

Kidding, of course.

But with Louie kidding *back?*

It seemed like it.

"Now I know why nobody ever noticed the difference," Louie said, returning the notes to his pocket.

"Difference?" said Bob.

"Yer," said Louie. "When your lot went on strike for six weeks."

As Smitty said shortly afterwards, "If *we* kidded around like that, we'd get the chop."

But Pat didn't mind.

Somehow the fact that Louie could joke at all about those notes was reassuring. At least it showed he wasn't really sore at her any more.

So long as there was no more snow, of course.

And so long as she caused no more delays.

Alas! Poor Pat!

Ten minutes later that's just what she did do.

Chapter
Seventeen

Santa
Is Missing

It happened in a much less densely populated part of
Wailey Heights. They had reached the farther limits by
now, beyond the end of the bus route and over the crest
of the hill. The houses here were wider apart, each in its
own spacious yard, and surrounded—British style—by
thick hedges. There was also a big school here, with playing fields. Because it was closed for the holidays, it helped to
make the neighborhood seem almost deserted compared to
the rest of Wailey Heights.

One result of the wider spaces between houses was longer

journeys from the truck, and bigger loads for the sleds.

"But I'll tell you what," Louie said to Pat. "Seein' the sleds was your idea. You can deliver your load in one go. Number Thirty, Wailey Crescent."

After gaping at this burst of generosity (*Louie,* making it easy for *her!*), Pat switched to gaping at the load.

Nearly two dozen bottles. Plus a dozen large orange juice, jars of cream, and other extras.

"All of it? At one house?"

" 'S what I said."

Pat looked at the boys. They were grinning. Was this some kind of crazy prank? *Had* Louie started accepting nips of something stronger than coffee? Was he getting light-headed because they were nearly at the end of the route?

Tim explained. "That's right, Pat. It's a County Council foster home."

"A what?"

"Like an orphanage, but on a small scale."

"More homely," added Smitty. "About fifteen kids—mostly little. They—"

"When you've finished the lecture on the British welfare system, professor . . ."

Louie glowered Smitty into silence.

"And here," he said, lifting a huge round tin box from the back of the truck, "give 'em this. Compliments of the firm."

Pat stared at the label, crudely hand-written with a felt pen:

AUNT MABEL'S OLD-FASHIONED
ENGLISH TREACLE TOFFEE

It was one of Louie's special extras, and from the feel of it the tin was full.

"Gee!" she said. "That's very kind of you. Thanks—"

"What are *you* thanking me for?" growled Louie, giving her a suspicious glare. "Thinking of snitchin' a piece for yourself, are yer?"

Pat flushed. This man was impossible.

"I most certainly am not! All I—"

"Well get on with the delivery then. Before the milk turns sour."

So Pat hurried off, soon getting over her indignation, buoyant as ever. And as she turned into the driveway of the house, her spirits rose higher still. Even without being told, she could have guessed that this was a house filled with children. The yard was crowded with snowmen, in all sizes and conditions. There was also a message in snowballs, carefully studded on the wall of the garage:

WELCOME SANTY CLAWS

There were no children out there just then, though. But they weren't far away. From one of the windows on the first floor—steamed up, glowing, festooned with home-made paper chains, and spattered with blobs of cotton— came the sounds of a piano being thumped, and feet being stamped, and young voices being raised. Some seemed to be singing, some laughing, some just squealing. A party.

With such a big load to deliver, Pat wondered whether she ought to ring the doorbell and let them know it had arrived. Then, as the noise inside rose to a crescendo, she wondered if anyone would hear her even if she did ring.

She was just going to give it a try anyway, when the

door opened.

"Thank goodness you—oh!"

A large round-faced woman in a red dress and a yellow paper hat stood there. The hat had CUDDLE ME QUICK WHILE YOU HAVE THE CHANCE written on it.

The broad smile on the round face suddenly straightened.

The shine in the eyes suddenly faded.

"Oh, I'm sorry . . . it's the milk . . . I—I thought it was someone else."

After the crescendo, there had been a kind of buzzing silence from behind her. Now it was broken. The piano was thumped again, even harder, but slower, and about fifteen young voices, wobbling and shaking with excitement, began to sing:

> "Happy Christmas to you,
> Happy Christmas to you,
> Happy Christmas, dear Santa,
> Happy Christmas to yoooo!"

Then clapping and cheering.

The woman looked as if she was ready to burst into tears.

"Is something wrong?" asked Pat. She glanced at the load. "Is there something missing—?"

"Oh, no . . . well . . . yes." The woman glanced over her shoulder as another chorus of "Happy Christmas" started up. A girl not much older than Pat came into the hallway.

"Aw! Isn't he here *yet?* They'll go mad in there—"

"Go back in, Sue. Tell Jacqueline to keep on playing,

keep on . . . oh dear!"

Again the woman looked like breaking down, as the girl returned to the party.

"Is there anything *I* can do?" asked Pat, still wondering what it was all about.

The woman shook her head, causing the paper hat to tilt over one eye. She pushed it back and sighed.

"No, love. I'm afraid there isn't. It's Santa, you see. They've been expecting him over an hour already. When I saw a movement out of the window I thought, Oh at last! But it was you. Not him."

"Santa? Santa *Claus?*"

"Yes. My husband. He was going to do it. He was coming home early specially. We've got the Santa costume all ready in the garage. He was going to arrive while they were all busy eating. I—I *told* them he was coming. Just to give them something extra to look forward to. And now—oh dear!"

"But surely he hasn't forgotten?"

"No. Of course not. My Bert was looking forward to it just as much as they were. But it must have been that blizzard. He's a long-distance bus driver, you see, and it must have held him up."

This was holding Pat up too. But that couldn't be helped. Not in a case like this.

As the third chorus of Santa's welcome was roared out, she made up her mind.

"Well look, why don't I—?"

But the woman was shaking her head. She must have thought of that already.

"You're too little, dear. My Bert's a tall man, and the costume was made specially for him. You wouldn't look right. Besides, your voice . . . and your cheeks . . . No. They'd spot it straight away . . . and . . ."

Pat wasn't listening. Her eyes had suddenly lit up.

"A *man,* hey? A *tall* man? . . . Ma'am, your troubles are over. Just stay right there. I'll be right back."

And leaving the sled at the door, still loaded, she went scampering and slithering back to the truck.

Chapter Eighteen

Santa LOUIE?

"Yer *what?*"

Louie looked outraged. Absolutely outraged.

He'd already been getting a little uptight at Pat's lateness in returning. Already he'd reached the stage of rolling up his right sleeve and having a good scratch at the N.D.D. initials tattooed there.

Pat's smile began to freeze just as the woman's had done. It was all at once dawning on her that Louie's donation to the kids of a box of treacle toffee was one thing, but asking him to spend a precious half hour with them was quite another. Especially in the role of Santa Claus.

He looked as if she'd asked him for a gallon of his blood. Or his last cigarette.

Tim suddenly found one of the truck's rear tires very interesting. Smitty rolled his eyes as if he'd seen, somewhere among the thick clouds, a glimpse of a U.F.O. and was wishing he were aboard.

"Now let's get this straight," said Louie. "You actually *promised* the woman? . . . You gone off yer nut or something? Eh? Miss! I'm speaking to yer!"

Poor Pat was having a problem keeping the tears back. But she managed to stammer out the reason why she'd made the promise. The circumstances. The urgency.

Louie relaxed a little. He still looked like an angry cat about to pounce on a sparrow that had been annoying it beyond endurance. But by comparison with what he'd been like a minute earlier—yes—relaxed a little.

He glanced at his watch. He glanced at the back of the truck and the few deliveries still to be made. He glanced at the sky.

Then he sighed, taking in sparks as well as smoke.

"Go on, then!" he grunted. "I'll give 'em ten minutes. Just ten minutes and no more."

Gratefully, Pat led the way.

Gleefully, Tim and Smitty came up in the rear.

"This," murmured Tim, "I must see."

"Yes," whispered Smitty, "but for Pete's sake don't let him see you grinning!"

But even Smitty couldn't control his grin in the garage, two minutes later, as the overjoyed woman helped Louie into his robes.

"You'll never know what this means to us, Mr. Lay. . . ."

"Yer, wuff. Luff gerruff wiff uff."

Louie's actual words were: "Yer, well. Let's get on with it." But just then Pat was fitting the massive white beard to his face.

"You look just right!" said the woman. "My Bert couldn't have looked better."

Well. Maybe. Maybe not.

Maybe Bert *was* as beady-eyed as Louie, at that. Long-distance bus driving can get you that way.

Maybe he was just as morose looking too.

On the other hand, he might have come much closer to the plump, red-cheeked, twinkling old jolly that Santa Claus is usually made to look. It might have been that the woman was just being polite.

But the beard helped, once it was on straight.

"So long as you keep the hood well down over your eyes," said Pat anxiously, as Louie hefted the sack of gifts as if he were going to clobber someone with it.

"And you take—" began Tim.

But it was too late.

Louie gave a yelp and the woman screamed and Smitty had the presence of mind to grab a handful of snow from the doorway and slap it into Louie's face.

Tim had begun to say, "And take the cigarette out of your mouth."

But Louie had already spit it out, the moment he felt the mustache begin to sizzle.

"Are you all right?" Pat asked.

Louie nodded.

The mustache and beard looked a little brown around the edges of the mouth, but the fire was out and the flames hadn't penetrated far enough to do any damage.

"Is this"—he nearly choked as a few charred hair tips were sucked in—"is *this* thing all right?"

"It'll do," said Smitty. "If any of the kids asks why your beard's gone a bit brown round the mouth, tell 'em you've just been eating stewed prunes."

Louie glared and then swept out.

"We're wastin' time!" he snarled.

Tim had to go into a corner of the garage to let some of his laughter escape in gasps, before it killed him.

But all anger, anxiety, and agony were dissolved when Santa Louie entered that room. The singing suddenly ceased. A great gusty gasp took its place. Fifteen pairs of eyes took on an even brighter sparkle. The girl at the piano nearly swooned with relief.

And then they cheered.

Again and again and again, shaking the lights and the colored bells on the Christmas tree, bringing down a sprig of holly from the overhead lamp, causing one end of a chain of paper lanterns to drop from the wall and drape itself over Louie's shoulders.

The matron held up her hands.

"Yes, children . . . yes . . . yes . . . thank you . . . he's here . . . he hasn't much time because the snow's been holding him up . . . and he mustn't keep other children waiting too long either, must he?"

"We waited!" said a little girl with wild red hair and critical eyes.

"Yes, Julie . . . but . . . well . . . anyway, here he is.

142

But before he gives out the presents, maybe he'd like to say a few words himself. Santa?"

Now you can't blame the woman. This is what she'd been rehearsing with her husband for weeks. The man had written for himself a little rhyming speech which went:

> It gives me joy,
> This Christmas Eve,
> To come among you here,
> To bring my sack and—

But that doesn't matter. Louie didn't know about any speech, rhyming or otherwise. And Louie soon made it plain that he didn't want to know, either.

Casting a glare at the woman that flashed even in the shadows of the hood, he cleared his throat.

"Well . . . huh . . . yuh . . . humph . . ."

Not the beard this time. There was plenty of room around the mouth, especially after the fire.

No.

Suddenly Pat realized. Louie had stagefright!

Louie! The man who prided himself on being able to deliver anything from milk to mushrooms—*Louie couldn't deliver a speech!*

Well, she'd gotten him into this. She was therefore the one to try and help him out.

"Excuse me," she said, stepping in front of Louie, "but Santa's not good at speaking English."

"Who're you?" said little Julie, in a hard voice.

"Me? I—I'm his secretary."

The kids looked interested.

In her bright orange parka and with her strange (to

them) American accent, she looked as if she could have been just that.

"And the problem is," continued Pat, "that he's lived so long among the Eskimos he only talks their language. He can *understand* English, but he can only talk back in Eskimo. Right, L—er—Santa?"

"Yerk kuh kuh!" grunted Louie, choking again, furious at the extra delay.

"There you are," said Pat. "That's Eskimo for 'Yes, alas, I am afraid you're right!' But don't worry, kids. If you'll just step up and get your gifts when your names are called, I'll do any translating."

And that's the way it went.

Most of the kids, especially the littlest, were too awed and thrilled to speak as they came up to collect their presents, so that was all right.

But when any of the older ones had a question or a comment, Pat was able to handle it. For example:

CHILD: "You won't forget to come tonight, will you?"

LOUIE: "Gerrumph cah gat!"

PAT: "He says, 'Of course I won't, you dear little boy!' "

And so on.

Only with the last child was there any trouble.

Julie.

Since at least twenty-five minutes had elapsed since Louie had put on the robes, he was beginning to get restive. And as Julie approached he had a scratch at his arm.

"Hey!" she said. "What's that, Santa?"

"Yek!"

"He says, 'What is what, my dear?' "

"That writing on his arm. N.D.D. it says."

Tim and Smitty, back over by the door, looked at each other and groaned. This could give the whole game away.

All sorts of people had made all sorts of cracks about those initials on Louie's arm. Some said the letters stood for Now Drop Dead. Others said it was a reference to the boniness of Louie's arm and meant Nice Dog's Dinner. But everyone knew it was really New Day Dairies.

Would it take long for Julie to catch on?

Again Pat came to the rescue.

"Yes," she said. "N.D.D. It's a reminder. When Santa first started, he used to drop the presents down chimneys. Or toss them to the foot of the Christmas trees like a boy delivering papers. Being in a hurry, you know. So many children to visit in such a short time. But then he started getting complaints. Dolls were getting broken. A hand here. A nose there. So when Santa heard about it, he had these letters printed on his arm to remind him. 'Never—' "

"Yes," interrupted Julie, nodding, satisfied. " 'Never Drop Dolls.' "

A bright kid, Julie.

And to show she really wasn't as distrustful as she may have sounded, she stepped forward and slapped a big wet smacking kiss on Santa's left cheek.

"If any of this gets around," said Louie on the way back to the truck, "I'll know who's blabbed!"

"Yes, sir," murmured Pat, subdued but still bubbling.

"And if anybody even *mentions* it," continued Louie, glaring at Smitty and Tim, "even among ourselves—he'll

—chuck!"

Louie had coughed, taking too fierce a drag at the cigarette he'd had to go without for so long.

"What's that?" asked Smitty, politely.

"That's Eskimo for 'he'll get the chop!' " said Louie, with another grim look at Pat.

And he would have looked grimmer still if he'd known that they hadn't yet finished with delays.

Chapter Nineteen

The Curious Behavior of the Temporary Christmas Mailman

The trouble with delays, as Louie well knew, is this: One leads to another.

Take that Christmas Eve for example.

The delay over Pat's "souvenirs" in the morning led to the New Day crew's meeting up with the Rely-On-Us crew at an ideal spot for a snowfight. The snowfight led to Kelly's big broken leg act. And Kelly's big broken leg act plus the earlier delays led to the New Day crew's being caught well and truly, slap-bang, in the blizzard.

Right?

Right.

Then the blizzard caused them to be at least two hours

late starting the second half of the route. True, they would have come up against the blizzard at some time whichever half of the route they were on. But with a bit of luck and without those early delays they could have been having their lunch break during the worst of it.

So let's say it put them one hour behind instead of two. Even that would have made a difference. If Pat had arrived at the foster home an hour earlier, the woman wouldn't have been so anxious. And if she hadn't been so anxious, Louie wouldn't have been asked to stand in for Santa. And if they hadn't been held up a half hour over that (putting them one and a half hours behind schedule), Pat would never have spotted the Curious Behavior of the Temporary Christmas Mailman.

You could say, of course, that it was a good thing they *were* held up in some cases. It was certainly a good thing for those foster-home kids that Pat arrived when she did. And it was an even better thing for all the people who'd been suffering from the Curious Behavior of the Temporary Christmas Mailman.

But hold it. We're going too fast.

Those who never read about it in the newspapers at the time will be saying *"What* Curious Behavior? *What* Temporary Christmas Mailman?"

It happened in the same part of Wailey Heights. The quieter part. The part with the wider gaps between houses, and taller hedges, and fewer people around. It happened in the perfect neighborhood for any Temporary Christmas Mailman who wanted to Behave Curiously.

Not that he really was a T.C.M. That was just his cover. But it had Pat fooled at first. Louie's sparring partner,

Bob, was a regular mailman, with a regular mailman's uniform. Being Christmas, however, the post office had hired temporary help, men and women in ordinary clothes, with special armbands.

The man that Pat saw behaving curiously had just such an armband. He also had a reddish-brown regulation mail sack over his shoulder. So at once she told herself, "Ah! That's a temporary Christmas mailman. . . . But, good heavens, what *is* he doing?"

Pat was delivering at the back door of a large house. Tim had warned her.

"Watch it. That's one of the Watchems. One of the complainers. Whatever you do, don't leave their milk on the front doorstep."

So there she was, around the back, when she heard the whistle. A sweet piping whistle, piercing the frosty stillness.

No. Not the T.C.M. Just a robin.

But Pat wasn't familiar with the British robin, which is much smaller and cuter than the American variety, so she turned to study it.

It was on some railings at the bottom of the yard. And beyond it were the backs of other houses. And *that's* when she saw the T.C.M.

Standing by the french windows of one of those houses. Bending. Cupping his free hand and looking into the unlit room.

"How polite the British are!" she thought then. "With certain exceptions, of course," she added, thinking of Louie. "But here is this temporary mailman, not even a regular. Yet does he hurry on his way when no one answers his ring at the front door? No, sir. He goes around to the back to make sure."

She watched discreetly, not wanting to appear nosy, but truly interested in the manners of another country. Maybe she could add this to her article for the school magazine.

She stepped to the corner, so that the man wouldn't see her if he glanced over his shoulder, and thus be embarrassed.

And now she marveled at his patience. No lusty pounding on that glass door. No loud hollering. And no question of just dumping the parcel he had for them in the snow on the doorstep.

No, sir, again.

He was trying his best. Patiently. Persistently. Politely.

Just seeming to scratch at that back door, timidly rubbing it instead of banging. Simply—

Then, as the glass faintly tinkled on the floor inside, and the man darted a look over his shoulder, so at last did the true meaning of what she'd been witnessing tinkle to the floor of Pat's mind.

She herself had darted back, only just in time.

"The rat!" she gasped. "He's breaking in! On Christmas Eve!"

Even the robin seemed shocked, blushing for shame.

She ran around to the front and rang the doorbell at the house where she was making her delivery. She wanted to ask them to call the police, keep watch, come and investigate with her.

But there was no reply, so there was nothing else for it but to run back to the truck and get Louie and the boys.

Surprisingly, Louie wasn't the least bit annoyed at this

delay. Angry, yes. But not with her.

"That's one of our customer's houses!" he said. "They've gone away for Christmas. Asked me to keep an eye on the place!"

Already he was hurrying to the scene.

"Not you, Smitty. You find a phone. Get the police. . . . Tim, Pat—you two get round the front of the house. Then if I flush him out that way, tail him. Don't let him out of yer sight!"

So Pat and Tim found themselves in the front street.

"That's the one," said Tim. "The one with 'Ash View' on the gate. You stay this side, I'll go that. Then whichever way he bolts we can be after him quick."

Even as Tim ran to take up his station, there came a muffled roar from over the hedge, followed by the slam of a door and skidding footsteps.

Then the man appeared: white-faced, wild-eyed, frightened, but still with the sack on his back. He also had something else under his arm—a large silver cup, a trophy he must have snatched up when Louie surprised him.

"Stay where you are!" cried Tim. "You won't get away with it!"

"The police are already on their way!" shouted Pat, from her side.

Suddenly the door slammed again.

The man made up his mind.

With Louie behind him, a sturdy-looking boy to his right, and a slim young girl to his left, the scoundrel didn't need a computer to prompt him which way to run.

"Outa my way!" he snarled, heading straight for Pat.

He had to do that—head straight for her—because only

a narrow track had been cleared on the sidewalk and she was on it. But no doubt he expected her to dodge to one side.

Well, Pat did no such thing.

She simply stood her ground, not even bracing herself. Her shoulders were slumped and her arms were slack and to anyone who knew nothing about judo she might simply have been lounging around, waiting for a bus.

The thief knew nothing about judo.

"I said get out the way!" he snarled, slowing a little as he came up to the girl.

And, because his arms were full, the scoundrel swung his foot.

Yes, he did. He swung a size-10 rubber boot, itself all asnarl with metal cleats, at this slip of a girl in the orange parka.

And that's all Pat needed.

Quickly, almost daintily, she grasped that foot just above the heel. Then, in the same movement, she executed a graceful little pirouette that would have done credit to the prima ballerina in the "Dance of the Sugar Plum Fairy." She also did other things: like using her free hand as a fulcrum and her left knee as a lever. Or maybe it was her right knee. Anyway, it was all over so quickly, as was the Temporary Christmas Mailman. Over her shoulder and head first into a mound of snow, where Tim and Louie joined him—Louie sitting on his back and Tim on his legs—until the police car, just turning into the street, came clinking up to them through the thick snow.

"Well, well, Louie!" said one of the policemen, getting out. "How you been?"

"Can't grumble," said Louie. "Long as the snow keeps off."

"Wouldn't be too sure about that," said the second cop.

"Oh?" said Louie.

"No," said the first cop.

"Glub!" gasped the thief, from the depths of the snow, reminding the two officers that they were there on business.

"What we got here then?" said one, yanking at the scruff of the man's neck.

"Oh, it's *you!*" said the second cop, seeing his face.

"Been after him a few days," said the first.

"Is he really a mailman?" asked Pat.

The policemen looked at her.

"Mailman, miss? You American?"

"Yes."

"We say 'postman' over here. What part you come from?"

"Connecticut," said Pat. "A place called—"

"Look!" cried the thief. "Either book me or let me go. But get these loonies off of my back!"

"Naw! He's not a postman, love," said the second cop. "This sack's just a blind. I bet it's full of old newspapers or—oho!" He was looking inside. "He's been using it to stash his winnings in! . . . You *have* been a busy little man, en't yer?" he said, hiking the thief to his feet.

The cops thanked Louie and the others again before they went off with their prisoner.

"You'll be following us down, I reckon?" said the driver.

"Where to?" said Louie.

"The station. Make your statements."

Louie shook his head.

"Not yet, mate. Still got a delivery to make."

"Well hurry up, then."

"Who're *you* tellin' to hurry up?"

"Keep your hair on, Lou! I don't mean for our sakes. I meant for yours. It's getting dark and there's this other blizzard on the way."

"What other blizzard?"

"The one we've been getting radio alerts about all afternoon. It's only about ten miles away now and it's coming up fast."

Chapter Twenty

The New Customer

"Still got a delivery, did you say?" Smitty asked, as they went back to the truck. "Which is that? I thought we'd finished with Wailey Heights. I thought that we'd—"

"Wailey Heights—yes!"

Louie was looking worried. The policemen's news had come as a bit of a shock to them all. The sky had been getting darker, but they'd been thinking this was more a result of the time than the weather.

"There's still that big country house," said Pat. "The one that you mentioned earlier. Is that what you're thinking about, Louie?"

"That's what I'm thinking about," said Louie.

"But Hardcastle Grange is two miles away!" said Smitty. He hadn't really forgotten about it. He'd only been hoping that Louie had. Or, rather, he'd been hoping that after the policemen's warning Louie would decide to forget the Grange. "You heard what the copper said. The storm—"

"Smitty," said Louie, and his voice was surprisingly calm, "if you want to pack up and go home, fair enough."

"Well, no, but—"

"In fact, if any of you want out, fair enough. It *is* only one delivery. It only needs one to handle it. Tim— you wanting to get off, too? Pat?"

"No," said Tim. "Well, yes—but no. I'll stick with you."

"I'm just raring to see a real old English mansion," said Pat. "But I guess Tim and Smitty are used to it, and if they want to quit—"

"Who asked *you?*" cried Smitty. "Who said anything about quitting? Who—?"

"I didn't mean it *that* way. I only—"

"Belt up!" Louie was beginning to lose that calm. They had reached the truck and he was already jerking the door open. "When I say it's fair enough, I mean it's fair enough. Only thing is, if you do decide to pack in, you'll have to make your own way back. But that shouldn't be any bother. The buses are running. . . . But me—I'm going to Hard-castle Grange."

The others ended the argument themselves—all three of them—simply by piling into the cab.

When they reached the farther side of the houses they'd been parked by, however, they began to have second thoughts. For now they had a clear view of the darkening countryside ahead of them.

The day's snow seemed to lie much deeper here.

"Look at the drifts!" gasped Smitty. "The hedges have been covered in places!"

"Nobody's given *this* road much of a plowing," said Tim.

"It's not all that bad," said Louie, going into bottom gear, nevertheless, and cutting down speed to a crawl while he tested the surface.

The trouble was the steepness. Below them was a narrow valley, with a single house at the bottom. Its lights seemed to offer more of a warning than a welcome. Like a buoy at sea.

"It might only need one to handle the delivery," said Smitty, suddenly sounding pleased. "But it's gonna take more than one to dig you out, if we get stuck down there."

He nudged Tim.

Tim grinned.

"Is it *still* fair enough if we get out and leave you to it, Louie?" he asked.

Louie didn't reply. He was too busy testing that surface.

"Where is the Grange?" asked Pat, peering into the valley. "Where the lights are?"

"Oh, it's not down *there!*" said Smitty. "That's the Brown Cow. A pub. That's only half way. No. See that clump of trees at the top over there, way over to the right?"

Pat could just make out a darker smudge where the violet-gray crest of the hill in front merged into the dirtier violet-gray of the sky.

"I think so—yes."

"Well it's just beyond there."

"Oh!"

She gulped. In that light, and with only the inn in the

valley showing any signs of life, and with another blizzard forecast, it looked a terribly long distance to go to make one delivery.

"Yes—'oh'!" said Smitty. "Hey! Louie! Are you sure it's worth it? Just *one* delivery. I mean is it worth getting the van stuck really good, maybe snowed over and abandoned, maybe out of service for *days?*"

Louie grunted. He seemed to have grown very thoughtful in the last few minutes.

"Worth it?" he murmured, still peering ahead at the snow on the road, sparkling in the headlights. "No."

"Well then," said Tim, "why don't we just turn round at the bottom while we've the chance?"

"Yes," said Pat. "Please don't do this just for me, Louie. I'll be in England for another week. There's still time to see a real old English—"

"Who said anything about doin' it for *you?"* growled Louie.

Pat flared. She was suddenly feeling the strain of the longest day of her life.

"Well why *are* we going there then? You've just said yourself that it's not worth it. Not in these conditions."

"Nothing to do with 'worth it,'" said Louie. "It's just that there's no choice. Those folks up there are depending on us. There's only the gardener and his wife. This might be the last chance of getting milk to them for days."

Nobody said anything. They were all too busy watching the first few flakes of what could be the next blizzard slowly dancing out there in the beams of the headlights. The boys were too busy making the sort of calculation

Pat was making, which was this:

> Will it really start in earnest by the time we reach the bottom? And if so, will it be bad enough to make Louie change his mind? And if he does change his mind, will it be soon enough for us to get back up here before the road becomes impassable?

Louie broke the silence.

"Did I tell you *why* the gardener's wife's not been so well lately?"

Smitty cleared his throat, rolled his eyes, squirmed a little. "Well—er—no—but—well—"

"No. You didn't *need* no telling, did yer? Either of yer?"

"Er—no—I suppose . . ."

Now it was Tim doing the squirming.

Pat was puzzled until Louie snapped, "What you both wriggling about for? It happens to all of us, doesn't it? *You* were born, *he* was born, *she* was born." Louie coughed. "Even *I* had to be born. Once upon a time. I reckon."

"Gosh!" said Pat, suddenly realizing what he was talking about. "You mean the lady's going to have a *baby?*"

Louie sniffed.

"Well, yer . . . You could put it like that. Way I see it though is this. The lady's having a *new customer*. When that kid arrives it'll mean seven extra pintsa milk a week. At least. Not to mention extra orange juice."

Smitty opened his mouth, then changed his mind, and

sighed, and rolled his eyes, and shook his head, and shrugged his shoulders.

"Well, anyway," murmured Tim, "it seems to have stopped snowing again. Must have been just a flurry."

"Yes," said Pat. "Thank goodness!"

But she wasn't thinking of their own safety or comfort any more. She wasn't thinking of how tired she was. She wasn't even thinking of her chances of seeing her first old English mansion on a frosty Christmas Eve.

She was thinking of that woman up there, and what the sound of the truck's engine and the rattle of bottles would mean to her right now.

Chapter Twenty-one

The Ghost of Hardcastle Grange?

Even without any further fall of snow, the climb up the opposite hillside was hard enough.

The road there was more twisting. At some of the sharp bends there had been drifting across the whole width. Very few other vehicles seemed to have been that way in the past four or five hours. If any.

Three times the New Day crew had to stop and use the shovels and spread sand and salt and cinders. And on the last of those three times even that treatment looked like being insufficient, when the back wheels started spinning.

That's when Louie's short thick planks came in handy.

"The only thing we haven't used is the blowtorch," said Smitty, as they went on their way.

"There's time yet!" was all Louie grunted.

The others said nothing. After three sessions with shovels, there wasn't much breath in them with which to say anything. Besides, they were beginning to get very uneasy. If that blizzard *did* hit them . . .

Pat didn't like to think about it.

They were near the top now, anyway. The road was flattening out some. Looking out away from the dazzle in front of them, she saw that it was almost dark. She twisted around, peering through the back window. It was blocked by crates of empties. But away behind Louie's head and out of the side window she kept catching a reddish glow in the sky, silhouetting a dark long hump that was studded with lights here and there along the top.

She guessed it was the hill they had come from. The lights would be those in the quieter fringe area of Wailey Heights. The glow would be coming from the rest of the town, beyond that. Civilization. Warm rooms. Christmas trees. Parties. It seemed an awful long way away now. Almost as remote as New England itself.

"We haven't passed the lane where we turn off for the Grange, have we?" asked Tim. "I mean in all this snow it might—"

"Nergh!" said Louie. " 'S here now."

There was a signpost, part of its lettering wiped out under frozen snow.

HARD ⁄ . . . . RA . GE

"That's what I'll be in," said Smitty "A *very* hard rage. If we get stuck along—oh, *no!*"

The truck had taken the turning all right. By a trick of the wind, the opening to the lane had been swept more or less bare. But it *was* only the opening.

Louie brought the truck to a stop with its front wheels deep in snow. Ahead of them, for as far as the beams were cast, the lights revealed more snow. And nothing but snow. Apart from the dark bristling upper twigs of a hedgerow on the left—the only indication of the course of the lane.

What made it look worse were the drifts every few yards, swept up like curtains to reach and cover the top of the hedge at those points. The front fender was jammed in one now. Maybe between drifts it wasn't too bad, but . . .

"We'll never get the van on there!" groaned Smitty, looking readier for a good hard cry than the hard rage he'd been threatening.

"And digging through those drifts," said Tim, "it would take us all night."

"Even the sleds won't be much use along there," said Pat, wistfully.

"So we'll walk it," said Louie, lighting a fresh cigarette and throwing the old one to fall with a fizz in the snow. "And we'll *carry* the stuff," he added, in answer to Pat's comment.

She tried to make out what was beyond the dazzle of the lights. Other than snow, of course. She thought she could just make out a darker patch—but no cheerful rows of windows blazing out into the night, as she'd always imagined an old English country house on Christmas Eve. Not even a single cheerful window. Not a glimmer.

"How far is it?" she asked.

"Oh, only about a mile and a half!" said Smitty.

"Don't talk wet!" snapped Louie.

"It'll seem it!" sighed Smitty.

"Cut the quacking and gimme a hand," said Louie, getting out. "I want one of those empty sacks. . . ."

They got out reluctantly, catching their breath in the cold after the warmth of the cab.

"I'll stow the delivery in here," Louie was muttering, as much to himself as to anyone else. "Be safer than a hand-crate in this lot. . . . Come on, one of yer! Hold this sack open."

Tim was there first.

Smitty flapped his arms miserably. Probably his Latin blood was feeling the cold more. Even so, Pat's New England blood wasn't exactly having a winter carnival. She stamped her feet.

An owl hooted—and down went the temperature of her blood another two degrees.

But there was pleasure, too, in the shiver she felt on hearing that sound.

"Hey!" she said to Smitty, while Louie stuffed bottles into the sack and muttered soft curses when Tim failed to keep it wide enough. "This Hardcastle Grange. It wouldn't have a ghost, would it?"

"Yes," said Smitty, without a flicker of hesitation. "Walks along this very lane. Every Christmas Eve. Right, Tim?"

"What?"

"Ghost of Hardcastle Grange."

"Oh! Yes!" Tim brightened up. "It's got three heads. Two on its shoulders and a spare under its arm."

"Ghost of a milkman," said Smitty, warming to the subject if to nothing else. "He got lost in a blizzard. The *stupido* would insist on making his delivery. Exactly one hundred years—"

"There'll be a coupla milkman's helpers' ghosts after tonight if you don't belt up. Will yer keep that sack straight, you! How many more—"

Louie broke off.

With good reason.

Wafting across his words, more dismal than the sound of the wind that carried it, there had come a moaning.

Faint, but unmistakable.

"Whu-what was *that?*" said Pat.

"I—wasn't it—could it have been the wind?" asked Tim, with something in his voice that said he was afraid he knew the answer, and it was No.

"It didn't sound like the wind to me," said Smitty, his eyes flashing in the reflected light as they rolled.

Louie had been talking at the time. He wasn't so sure about the direction. His face glowed angrily as he pulled on his cigarette and looked at the others.

"If one of you is playing tricks, it'll be—"

Again he stopped.

Again the moaning.

This time there was no doubt about whether or not it was the wind. Wind nothing! And this time even Louie could tell where it came from. Somewhere behind him.

And now the moaning persisted. It began to form words. Not just "Oh!" or "Hee!" The wind can make those words all right. But these were ghostly extensions of "Oh!" and "Hee!" which mainly ran to,

"Oh-over . . . hee-here . . ."

Chapter
Twenty-two

Emergency

"It's coming from behind that second drift," said Pat. "Near the hedge . . . I think . . ."

The moaning had risen into a thin shriek. It sounded more like a tormented soul than ever. It seemed to sing of the place it had just come from.

"He-ell . . ." But this was only the beginning of another word it was trying to form. "He-ell-p . . . he-ellp me . . ."

"Come on!" grunted Louie, plunging through the first drift. "That's no ghost. That's a man. In trouble."

The others plunged after him, casting long grotesque

shadows in the beams of the truck's headlights.

Pat had been wrong.

It was the *third* drift along the lane.

But it *was* near the hedge, in the blue-black strip of shadow formed by the drift curtain, that they found the owner of the voice.

He'd been almost buried. Only his head, shoulders and arms were free. And in that dim light he looked every bit as eerie as the sort of ghost they'd been talking about. A kind of body-less ghost, Pat couldn't help thinking, as she peered over Tim's shoulder.

Louie was digging away with his hands, quickly but carefully, all around the man.

"You all right, mate?"

"My leg. Careful when . . . when you get down there. . . ."

"It's the gardener," Smitty told Pat, in a whisper.

"Don't worry. We're good at broken legs. Long as yer name's not Kelly." Louie was still scrabbling away. "Here!" He paused and took his cigarette from his mouth. "Have a drag on that while we see what to do."

The man accepted it in his mouth, then blew the smoke out in a small explosion.

"Never mind *me!* . . . Ouch!"

"Easy . . . Smitty—get a shovel. He's in the ditch. We're gonna have to dig a space out both ends of him. So we can maneuver him out of it."

The man's face was a bluey-white. His eyes had closed. The cigarette fell from his mouth. Louie picked it up and put it in his own again.

"Only fainted," he murmured. "Be all right . . . Come

on, Smitty! . . . Whassat?"

He nodded farther along the side of the hedge.

The removal of Smitty's shadow had revealed some-thing gleaming there, partly drifted over by the snow, but with a familiar look about it.

"Handlebars," said Tim. "A bike."

Louie nodded.

"Leave it. He won't be—"

The man was groaning again, blinking. The word "bike" seemed to have aroused him.

"I was carrying—carrying it—hoping the road would be . . ." Suddenly his shoulders jerked and his head came up.

"Look—please! Never mind *me!* It's the wife. . . . I think she's started . . . the baby. . . ."

"Clear a space there, just behind him," said Louie, when Smitty came up. "Yer—go on, mate. . . . The baby."

"I think . . . earlier than we expected . . ."

"Be careful, you dope! . . . Yer—I'm listening, mate."

"But the wires . . . the wires . . . you see!"

"What wires are those? . . . Now this side, Smitty."

"The telephone wires . . . down . . . blizzard . . . this morning. I was trying to . . . to get to the pub . . . down there . . . carrying my bike over these drifts . . . then . . . this."

"Yer, well, not to worry." Louie had now got the snow cleared from the whole length of the man. Smitty had scraped firm bases on the bottom of the ditch at either end of him. "I know you're not supposed to move a bloke with a suspected fracture. But then you're not supposed to leave him freeze to death either. Now, where d'you say it hurts most?"

"Ankle . . . ankle . . . but never mind me . . ."

"All in good time, mate. Me and young Doctor Kildare here—come on, Smitty, get that side—we're gonna make a chair. With our arms. All you do is sit on it. . . . These other two'll just ease you into position. . . . Tim, take his right arm, high up. . . . Pat, the left arm. . . ."

So, sliding about dangerously at first, then getting firmer footholds, they gradually eased the man into a sitting position, with Smitty's and Louie's clasped forearms already under him. And so, slowly, very carefully, they carried him back through the broken but still treacherous drift curtains to the truck, where they laid him across the seat.

"Right!" said Louie, over the man's weak protests. "Here's what we do. You two lads—that big green-and-red sled. The new one. Should go like a bird down that hill. If it doesn't, don't mess around. Dump it and run. Only get to the Brown Cow quick. Tell 'em to phone for an ambulance. Feller with a suspected fracture. Bad sprain at least. And a woman having a baby. Tell 'em where and tell 'em to look sharp. Now move." They moved and he turned to Pat. "You—stay here with him."

"But what about my wife?" wailed the man. The warmth of the cab seemed to have given him a short burst of strength. "What if she has the baby before they get here? Complications?"

Louie took a deep breath.

"Mister, I have delivered milk all my life. And besides milk, orange juice, nylons and watch repairs. I've even delivered horse-racing tips and mushrooms, in season. I've delivered all these and dozens more, and I've never let anybody down yet. So if there's a child to be delivered"—he took another deep breath and the glow of his cigarette brightened, lighting his cheekbones—"I'm yer man!"

He bent to the sack that he'd started to put the delivery in earlier.

"Just hold this for me," he told Pat.

Then he began piling extra things in—cans of fruit, jars of cream and honey and yogurt, more bottles of milk, packs of cookies, two bottles of sherry, a Christmas cake— practically everything that had been left over.

"They'll need more 'n their usual order," he muttered. "Specially if the blizzard comes on again."

He ended with a spare jar of elderberry wine. The sack was nearly full now.

"Right," he said. "That's me. You'll find some cigs in the glove compartment, if he wants to smoke. . . . Hey—and here!" He pulled out the jar of wine. "Second thoughts, this'll probably be more use right here. Try and get him to have a swig. It'll keep him warm and it'll keep him quiet. . . . See yer!"

"Are you sure—?" Pat began.

But Louie was already plodding knee-deep through the first drift, casting monstrous shadows with the sack over his shoulder.

Pat shrugged.

"Oh, well . . ."

She went to the cab and put her head in.

"Feeling any more comfortable now, sir? There are cigarettes in—"

"Does—does he know what to *do?*" groaned the man.

Pat frowned. That was what she'd been wondering. If Louie was as bad at delivering a baby as he was at delivering a speech, then—

But she shook the frown clear of her face.

"Well he *sounded* as if he knows what to do. And he knew what to do about you and your ankle and getting you out of the ditch and all. I mean he's really a very capable man is Mr. Lay. . . . Anyway, cheer up. It's usually a few hours before the baby starts coming out. The ambulance people will be here before anything drastic— Sir? You all right?"

Groaning deeply, the man was struggling to rise.

"But it *was* a few hours ago! It was only just after three when I started out. I—"

"Oh!"

Pat sounded shocked.

She was. This was something else again.

Then she made up her mind.

"Sir, just quiet down. Please. I see what you mean. Really I do. But I happen to know quite a bit about delivering babies myself. At Ward Ridge—but never mind that. Just believe me. . . . Now, if I leave you here, will you be—?"

"Go! Please!" The man was pushing her now, feebly but frantically. Most likely he'd never heard of Ward Ridge in his life before, let alone the versatile program of studies offered by the school there. But something in the girl's voice must have reassured him. "I'll be fine! Just go! Go!"

Pat went.

Chapter
Twenty-three

Good
King
Louielaus

Louie's Christmas tribulations had begun with a carol, the day before. Now, on Christmas Eve, they looked like reaching a climax with a carol. Then it had been "The Twelve Days of Christmas." Now it was "Good King Wenceslaus." Without music and without words. Or at least without the original words.

For that was how Pat came to see it, as she plunged after Louie along the drifted lane.

"Just like the page," she said to herself. "Following in his master's footsteps."

Except that they weren't exactly *foot*steps. Not all the

way. Crisp that snow might have been; deep—yes; but even—no. So in some places they were *knee*steps that she followed. In others they were *thigh*steps. In yet others they were *buttock*steps—with the dragging imprint of the sack brushing over them.

This was probably a good thing, in one respect. Once Pat was out of the light from the truck, she entered into a stretch of great darkness, in spite of the snow. Mere footsteps there might easily have been missed. Fortunately, it was only a short stretch, and with those great breaches in the snow-drift curtains to mark the way, it wasn't too bad. And after that, her eyes became more accustomed to the dimness.

And then, of course, dark or not, there was always sound to go on. The crunch of boots on the less deeply covered patches. The clink of bottles in the sack. The scraping of twigs as the sack brushed against frost-brittle shrubs. And the words that exploded from Louie from time to time.

Such words . . .

You couldn't blame the man. He didn't know a girl was following him. She made no attempt to let him know it, either. No discreet cough. No calling out of his name. Pat had decided not to announce herself until they reached the Grange. She wanted no delay caused by arguments out here in the snow, with Louie ordering her back to the truck and herself refusing. She wanted to spring her presence on him when it would be too late for such a dispute.

So. The words . . .

They weren't exactly the words that King Wenceslaus would have used. Not *Good* King Wenceslaus, anyway. But they weren't all that bad, either. Just rough around the edges. In fact, they helped to cheer Pat's way as well as guide it. They helped to warm her heart, transporting her in spirit 3,500 miles back home. The truth was that they reminded her of nothing and no one so much as her own dear father.

Louie came to an extra-thick drift, bringing him to a sudden stop; and Pat heard the word her father had used that time when he was in a hurry to get to the airport and the car got into an unexpected traffic jam on the Merrit Parkway.

Louie slid on a thinly covered but treacherously icy stretch, his black-shadowed shape doing all manner of pirouettes in an effort to keep upright; and Pat heard the phrase her father had used when the rug began to slide from under him on the too well-polished floor of the dining room last Thanksgiving, when, to the tune of "Yankee Doodle Dandy" on tapes, he was triumphantly bearing the turkey, fully trimmed and steaming hot, from the kitchen.

Louie came under a snow-laden branch of one of the fine oak trees in the Grange avenue, startling an owl there and causing it to take off so abruptly that about ten pounds of snow slid off—*scosh!*—onto Louie's head. Then Pat heard the identical expression her father had used the evening that part of the ceiling fell on him, showering him with plaster, just as he was about to produce a royal flush in a friendly game of poker.

Memories, memories . . .

But by now master and page were nearly at the Grange.

No blazing lights still. No sounds of merriment. Just a great long dark silent pile, with vague battlements that looked ready to receive Count Dracula. But there was one light, yes. Dim, diffused, around the side, coming from a curtained first-floor window near to a door marked: TRADES-MEN'S ENTRANCE.

Pat was close enough to see what it said, in the light reflected back from the snow. She guessed it was the British way of saying SERVICE ENTRANCE.

The time to declare herself had come.

"Louie!" she said softly, just as the milkman was reaching out with a key that the gardener must have given him.

He jumped, rattling all the bottles in the sack; and Pat heard the prayer her father had put forth the night when he was creeping in from a stag dinner and the cat had leaped onto his shoulder—a friendly gesture in the daylight, but deadly in the dark.

"What—what *you* doing here?" were Louie's next words.

Pat had it all ready. She spoke crisply, quickly, clearly.

"Well, for one thing, it's my only chance of seeing a real old-fashioned English mansion on Christmas Eve. . . . No, wait. . . . And for another, something tells me that lady in there might like another woman around at a time like this. . . . No, hear me out. . . . And for yet another"— Pat slowed down some, letting each word sink in, the way they'd taught her in the Junior Debating Class back home— *"have you had any experience of delivering children?"*

That pulled him up. His cigarette rolled from one side of his mouth to the other, glowing less strongly, as he chewed on *that* point.

"Well—yer," he said uneasily. "Back at the kennels. Where Janice works. My girl friend. I've sat with her many a night when one of the dogs has been having a litter.

Nothing to it."

Pat sighed. Relief. What a good decision she'd made, coming after him like this!

"Louie," she said, "master you may be in the milk business. But there are things you have to learn outside it."

"Like what?"

The cigarette jutted defiantly.

"Like it's very different when a human mother is having a baby. Some of the things a mother dog does for herself—remember them?"

"Yer. So?"

"The doctor or midwife has to do them for the human mother."

"Eh?!"

The cigarette nearly fell out.

"Yes, Louie. Yes, indeed."

"But—here! How do *you* know? You're only a *kid!* You—"

"Just another of the things they teach us at Ward Ridge. In biology. And as an aunt—with two older married sisters . . . But we're wasting time. Do I get to go in? Or do I have to use my judo lessons?"

The last threat was nothing to Louie. (He was, as a matter of fact, a secret Blue Belt himself, with two red stripes.) In fact, he didn't even hear it, so busy was he thinking about what Pat had said already about a midwife's duties. And that was enough for him.

His reply was simply to open the door, step aside, and mumble, "You go first."

Then Pat heard groans for the second time that evening and knew from the sound of them that she'd arrived not a minute too soon.

"We'll need lots of hot water," she said over her shoulder. "Think you can locate the kitchen?"

"I'm on my way—" came Louie's answer. And so impressed was he by her manner that, after only the slightest of pauses and without a trace of sarcasm, he added one more word, "Nurse."

Chapter
Twenty-four

Christmas
Caravan

Meantime—rough time.

That's what Tim and Smitty had been having.

First of all, the sled failed to work.

After leaving the truck, they had run all the way to the point in the road where it began to dip sharply. Then, "Right!" said Smitty. "You get behind me. I'll steer. Ready? . . . He-e-e-e-re we go!"

And the-e-e-ere they went. At what seemed like the speed of sound, crouched down there in the darkness.

For all of two hundred feet.

That was the distance to the first sharp bend.

In the dark it hadn't looked all that sharp, and up they went, climbing the snow-covered bank. Up, up, up the bank instead of around that bend and down, down, down the road.

It really seemed as if that sled was determined to climb a big old tree, growing out of the bank at that corner. In fact, it did make quite good progress up the trunk, after throwing Tim and Smitty off headlong into the deep drifted snow there. That sled—that new green-and-red sled—may not have gone down the hill "like a bird," as Louie had predicted, but it certainly went up the tree like one. Just as if it thought it was Woody Woodpecker with a two-pronged beak.

When it found it couldn't make it, back it fell, just missing the boys. The two prongs, the front runners, had been badly bent.

"We'll never get anywhere on this now!" said Tim.

"So we do what Louie said," Smitty replied.

"What was that?"

"We dump it and run instead."

So they dumped it and ran. Or slithered and skidded might be a more accurate way of putting it. All the way down to the Brown Cow, anyway.

Then they hit the next rough patch, when the owner nearly set the dogs onto them.

"We're not open!" bellowed a voice above the barking. "Not till six o'clock."

"You've got to let us in!" cried Smitty, still hammering at the door.

"Got to?" demanded the owner. "Who d'you think you are?"

"We deliver the milk—"

"Hargh!" roared the voice, causing the dogs to bark louder. "Not here you didn't. Not this morning when we needed it. You let us down good and proper!"

That's when it seemed as if he was going to open up just to set the dogs on them.

But when Smitty explained they were New Day deliverers and not Rely-On-Us, both man and dogs calmed down some. And when the boys went on to explain about the gardener with the injured leg, and his wife, the innkeeper couldn't have been more helpful. He even offered them glasses of hot green-ginger wine while Smitty tried to use the phone.

And that was the next rough patch.

Trying to use the phone.

No; not trying to get through to the Ambulance Service. That was smooth enough. There had been no lines blown down in the valley. The rough patch came after Smitty had obtained the number he'd dialed.

"Duty driver," said a strangely familiar voice.

"Quick!" said Smitty. "We're out at the Brown Cow, between Wailey Heights and Hardcastle Grange. There's a man up at the turn-off to the Grange and he's—"

"Just a minute!" said the driver. "Don't I recognize the voice? You're one of the New Day Dairies delivery lads, aren't you?"

"That's right. But listen. This man—the gardener at the Grange—he's—"

"And you're the one who called us this morning, aren't you?"

"Am I? I mean—oh, yes! Yes. Well. I suppose—"

"Yes! I *thought* so. . . . Go on, sonny. What is it *this* time?"

"Well we think the man might have a broken leg, but—"

"Not *another* broken leg? Listen—you tell that sandy-haired pal of yours that this is Christmas Eve, not April Fools day."

"What sandy-haired pal?"

"That newspaper kid you said had a broken leg this morning. Regular comedian, he is. He's been going around town saying how you and him made a right pair of clowns out of us. How we couldn't tell a broken leg from a banana split. How—"

"What is it?" asked Tim, as Smitty held the phone away from his ear, rolling his eyes and looking pained.

"That Quentin Kelly again! *Mamma mia!* Something oughta be done about him. . . . Yes, sir!"

"You listening?" the man was saying. "If it wasn't Christmas—"

"Are *you* listening?" Smitty cut in—and his tone must have pulled the man up. "Because it's not just the gardener, it's his wife. She's having a baby and she's all alone and there might be complications and . . ."

After that, the ambulance man was all attention. He remembered the woman as an outpatient at the hospital—and now he believed everything Smitty was telling him. What was more, he did better than just set out in the ambulance with his partner. He informed the doctor who'd been attending to the woman at the hospital, and he said he'd come along too. Then the driver got in touch with the police about the emergency, and they agreed to detail a patrol car to escort the ambulance. And the police, knowing the conditions out there, had the foresight to call out a special light snowplow.

So it came to pass that a complete motorcade arrived at the Brown Cow about twenty minutes later: snowplow, police car, ambulance. With red lights blinking and blue lights flashing and churned-up snow frothing and spuming in front, it looked almost festive, a Christmas caravan.

"And this time if you've been pulling our legs," said the ambulance driver as the boys got in with him, "it'll be instant arrest and Christmas Eve in the nick."

But he could tell from their faces that they weren't kidding. Nearly an hour had gone by since they'd left the truck and they were getting worried about what had been happening up there during that time. Even the driver's news that the threatened blizzard looked like skirting the area after all—even that didn't do much to relieve their anxiety. And now that they were just passengers, without anything to do, they felt that anxiety more keenly.

Once again it was slow going up that hill, even with the snowplow leading the way. Another precious ten minutes crawled by before they reached the top and the abandoned truck.

The ambulance men got out with a stretcher, while the police lit up the truck from behind, and the snowplow driver edged past and continued along the lane, getting on with the main task he'd come for.

Tim and Smitty and the doctor followed the ambulance men.

"Hello!" they heard the driver say. "What have we got

here?"

He hadn't even reached the truck.

"Yes," said his colleague. "I didn't expect one of *those* cases for another five hours at least."

They still hadn't reached the truck, but it wasn't hard for the boys to guess what they were talking about.

"No-o-ell! No-o-ell!"

More mournful than the groans of the ghost he'd first sounded like, came the tones of the gardener as he sang in the cab.

"Blimey!" said the driver, looking in. "I don't know about his leg yet, but *he's* smashed!"

"No-o-ell! No-o-ell! . . . Good evenin', gen'men. . . . *No-o-ell!"*

"What's *that* he's got there?" said the doctor.

Tim looked at Smitty. Smitty looked at Tim. The gardener was stretched on the seat they'd left him on. But now he was clutching a half-empty jar of Louie's elderberry wine, and there was no sign of Pat.

The gardener's pain had certainly been killed. But so had his memory. He couldn't tell them anything about the others. Wolves could have come and gobbled them up for all he knew. And he seemed to be under the impression that his wife had had a completely successful delivery, safe in the hospital somewhere.

"Triplets!" he murmured happily, nursing the bottle as they carried him into the ambulance. "All boys. Melchior, Caspar, 'n' Balsh- Balff- . . ."

He was still trying to pronounce the name Balthazzar when the rest of the caravan got under way again—at a much slower rate—in the wake of the hard-working plow.

"Santa Lucia!" cried Smitty, as they finally turned into the long oak-bordered avenue leading up to the Grange. "It's lit up *now* all right!"

It was. The place looked more like a huge liner than a house—a liner getting ready to sail on the midnight tide—with every light ablaze on every deck. Even the lanterns over the great front door did nothing to spoil this impression, for they simply made the steps there look like the ship's gangway.

"What's the idea of that, I wonder?" said Tim.

"It means that everything's O.K., what else?" said Smitty, bouncing in his seat in his eagerness.

"Or it could simply mean they want to light the way better, to get us to hurry up," said the driver grimly, with a quick glance back at the man on the stretcher, who was still trying to pronounce the name of the third eastern king as the doctor attended to his ankle.

All of a sudden, Tim wished they could do just that—hurry up—and now even Smitty wasn't looking so sure.

But the plow had its work to complete first, lights or no lights, and all the boys could do was sit tight, and hope and pray and wonder exactly what was going on behind those blazing windows.

Chapter Twenty-five

The Best Present of All

"Louie?"

Pat sounded troubled.

"What?"

"Will Lord Hardcastle *mind?*"

"Mind what?"

"Putting all the lights on. Every light in the house. Just to please *me*. Just to let me see a real old English country mansion all lit up on Christmas Eve?"

Louie and Pat were in the long main dining hall, under the shimmering blaze of a fine old crystal chandelier that had been converted to use electricity. Half a kilowatt of electricity, in fact. At that one point alone. Heaven only knew what the total cost would be. Only heaven knew at the moment, anyway. Lord Hardcastle would be getting to know later, of course. When the electricity bill came in.

"One," said Louie, "I didn't put all the lights on for you. I put 'em on to make sure. If the blizzard hits us and it's anything like this morning, the rescue team's gonna need every glimmer of light we can put out."

"Oh," said Pat, feeling a bit put down, yet also a little better. "I see."

"And two," said Louie, "it doesn't matter what *Lord* Hardcastle thinks." He'd put a slight jeer into that "Lord" bit. "Emergency like this."

Pat nodded. They were sitting at the long twenty-foot banqueting table, she at one end, Louie at the other, with the chandelier shimmering between them. Pat had one of the famous Hardcastle silver goblets in front of her. It was filled with orange juice. Louie had one of the even more famous Hardcastle golden goblets in front of him. It was filled with cheap sherry from his sack of goodies.

Pat gave a tired giggle.

"I bet he'd mind if he saw us sitting here like this though. Using his fancy goblets and all. The gardener only meant us to use the door key, not any of the other keys on the ring."

Louie snorted softly, spraying cigarette ash in a way that would have had the Hardcastle butler wincing, had he been present.

"Young Widdie? Mind us doing this? Not he! Pal of mine, young Widdie. Always asking me up for a drink. Never had time before. . . . Nargh! He'd be delighted."

"Young—er—Widdie?"

"Yer. Widdicombe Hardcastle."

"You mean Lord Hardcastle? Himself? A—a friend of yours?"

"Yer!" Louie took a swig from the golden goblet. Under the strong lights his eyes looked tired, but still alert. He seemed to be listening for something. Indeed, he *was* listening for something. Anxiously. Just as Pat was listening for something, though not so anxiously. "Young Widdie," Louie murmured. "One of the best crate stackers I ever had."

That made Pat forget for a moment what she'd been listening for. It made her choke a little on the sip of orange juice she'd just taken.

"Crate stackers? You mean he was—he—Lord *Hardcastle*—?"

"One of my helpers." Louie nodded. "Sure! Mind you, he wasn't a lord then. Not while his father was alive. Young Widdie was only an Honorable then. The Honorable Widdicombe Hardcastle. Yer."

"Well son of a gun!"

"No, son of a baron. Same thing in this case, though. Hard-nosed old feller, the old Lord. Comes up to me one morning. 'Lay,' he says, 'I been watching you.' 'Oh yer?' I said, ready to let him have it. 'Yes,' he says, 'and what I've seen I like.'"

Louie took a long drag at his cigarette.

"'Hello!' I thought. 'He's broke.' Some of these Lords are, y' know. 'He wants tick. He wants to put his bill on the slate.' That's what I thought when he said he liked what he'd seen of me."

Louie took another swig. His eyes were flitting still, and under the lights Pat could almost fancy she saw his ears twitch.

"You sure she's—?" he began.

Pat nodded.

"Don't worry about that. Just resting. Go on about Lord Hardcastle. The old Lord Hardcastle."

Louie gave the girl a beady look.

"Well, you seem to know what you're doing," he said.

Then he shrugged and continued, "Yes. Well. What the old buzzard really wanted was for me to give his son a job. Young Widdie. Due home from Eton. Long Easter holidays. 'The brat needs lickin' into shape!' says the old man. 'And I've given him a choice. Either go to Iceland on one of the Hardcastle trawlers, as a cabin boy, working eighteen hours a day, rough seas. Or get a job helping that milk deliveryman who comes here.'"

Louie's cigarette grinned slightly. One half circle.

"Widdie picked me. Passed the tests I gave him. He thought he was onto a soft touch. Heh! The old man knew what he was doing though. Before the first week was out that lad was *pleading* to be sent to Iceland. But he wasn't a bad kid. Guts. Soon buckled to. Joined us every holiday he had, after that."

"Well," said Pat, "I—"

Then she heard what *she'd* been listening for. The chugging of engines. Voices. Car doors slamming. Footsteps. More voices. The knocking at the main door.

"It's not locked!" she called, going toward it.

"What kept yer?" jeered Louie, as it swung open, and Tim, Smitty, two policemen, two ambulance men, and a worried-looking doctor came piling in, stamping the snow off their boots on a baronial doormat as big as a normal living-room rug.

"Where is she?" asked the doctor.

"She?" said Louie, and suddenly the fighting stags on his sweater seemed to break apart and make an honorable peace, as his chest swelled. *"They,* you mean? Don't yer?"

"Through here," said Pat, ushering the doctor into the dining hall and through it and out at the far door, ready open, near which Louie had been sitting, his ears pricked for the slightest sound of distress. Understandable, of course, since this was his first delivery of that kind of Christmas special. And understandable of Pat not to be so anxious—being the expert and knowing what kind of a job she had done.

"Magnificent!" said the doctor, coming into the dining hall after five minutes, followed by two very respectful-looking ambulance men. "Why, you even cleaned up! It's as if she'd had the child in a comfortable, fully-equipped—"

"Healthy?" asked Louie.

"Sound as a bell. A fine little chap."

"New Day only deliver the best," said Louie, pouring himself a drop more sherry.

Nearly everyone had goblets now. Tim and Smitty's were silver, as sparkling as their eyes. Tim had milk in his. So had Smitty, though—just to be a bit of a devil—he'd asked for and been given a dash of sherry with it. The policemen were having milk laced with medicinal brandy from their emergency kit. The ambulance men elected to have the same, and the doctor chose plain brandy, a good stiff shot, because he wasn't driving and most of his work had been done for him.

They were just about to drink to the baby's health when

a mournful howl came from outside.

"No-e-ell!"

It was more of a cry for help than a carol.

"Good heavens!" said the doctor. "The father! Bring him in. I was afraid that we might have had to keep him out of the way for a while. But thanks to the splendid work done by this gentleman and this young lady—"

"This young lady!" said Louie firmly. "It was all her doing."

Tim and Smitty looked at each other. For Louie to give credit to his helpers was rare enough. But to give *full* credit . . .

"Hey, now, come on!" said Pat. "You were a great help."

"Oh, yes!" said Louie. *"Very* great." He took another swig of sherry. Fatigue, lack of food, strain, relief—they were all combining with the drink to make him less alert, more relaxed. Tim and Smitty had never seen him like this. Why, he was actually smiling now. With his *mouth.* It was rather a crooked smile, but still . . . "You know what *I* did?" said Louie, suddenly fierce. "I—"

"He helped to keep me supplied with hot water!" said Pat firmly. "And a thousand other things. Without which I'd have been hopeless."

Louie glared at her.

She glared back.

Then Louie slowly shook his head and shrugged, and Pat knew she'd won.

For Louie *had* done what she'd just said. It was quite true. And as far as she was concerned there was absolutely no point in his making the confession he'd been about to make. Why, once he'd had a good night's sleep, he'd never forgive himself for having blurted it out in his fatigue. Or her, for letting him.

And what *was* this secret? What *had* Louie done, besides help Pat with hot water and so on? What *had* been his first act on reaching that bedside?

Louie (and this must never get any farther, this secret must never go beyond this point)—Louie, who'd been so sure of himself, who would certainly have ordered Pat back if she hadn't waited until they reached the Grange—Louie, the iron man, the terror of generation after generation of helpers—*Louie . . . had . . . fainted.*

There. Now eat this message and forget it.

Louie seemed to pull himself together after that exchange with Pat, suddenly aware of how near he'd been to making the awful confession. As the gardener was carried in to see his wife and son (and there was another man who'd suddenly pulled himself together, lying silent and seemingly sober now, white-faced on the stretcher, under the blazing lights, on his way to receive the best Christmas present he'd ever had in his life), Louie changed the subject.

"Did I dream it, or were you saying a while back that they *do* have milkmen in America?"

"Oh, sure!" said Pat. "There's one in the Ward Ridge area—"

"Ah! That place!" said Louie, shaking his head with grudging admiration.

"And in New York, also. In the city, I mean. Even there. My aunt lives in an apartment near Lincoln Center and I know for sure they deliver the milk door to door, because she's been complaining about people stealing it early in the morning, before she's had time to take it in."

"Now *that,*" said Louie, all alert and professional again, "we have ways of dealing with. Right, lads?"

They agreed. Even the policemen grinned, having heard of Louie's methods of combating this grave crime. True, had it not been Christmas Eve those cops might have scowled and told him that that was *their* job. But not tonight, of all nights. . . .

Then Pat had her idea.

"Say, why don't you come over and see for yourselves? . . . Next vacation? . . . All three of you? . . . Daddy will be so interested in meeting you. He'll fund the whole trip. Put it down to business. The exchange of marketing ideas."

"Why *not?*" cried Tim, joyfully.

"Pat, *cara mia,* you've just got yourself three house guests!" sang Smitty.

"Well, we'll have to see," grunted Louie. "And if we do go, I'm telling you now"—he looked grimly in turn at each of his helpers, the two regulars and the temporary—"it *will* be business. We *will* be studying how it's done over there. It *won't* be any picnic!"

That was enough for the boys and Pat.

They raised their goblets and clinked them.

"Here's to it!" they cried.

The fact that Louie hadn't said No was as good as a promise. And—business or no business, picnic or no picnic—they regarded that promise as the best Christmas present *they'd* ever had.

"Now, how about a carol?" said Smitty, bursting to celebrate.

"Sure, why not?" said Pat. "Which one?"

"Anything but 'Noël'!" said Tim.

"Let's leave the choice to our temporary host here," said one of the policemen, grinning at Louie.

Louie looked hunted.

"Yer—well . . ." Then he cleared his throat. "Uh—how about 'Tom Dooley'?"

E. W. HILDICK is the author of over forty books for children and teen-agers, five adult novels, and several critical books. Among his children's books are a number written especially for American readers, including *Manhattan Is Missing, The Doughnut Dropout, The Active-Enzyme Lemon-Freshened Junior High School Witch, Birdy Jones and the New York Heads,* and this book, and he has also adapted several of his best British books for children in this country. These include *Louie's SOS* and *Louie's Lot,* which in 1968 won the Diploma of Honor of the Hans Christian Andersen Award Committee as best children's book to come from Britain in the two years 1966–67. The popularity of his books extends far beyond the English-speaking world. Countries in which his works are enjoyed in translation include France, Germany, Portugal, Poland, Sweden, Italy, Denmark, Holland, Spain, Russia, Yugoslavia, and Iceland.

Before he began writing books, Mr. Hildick spent three years as a free-lance journalist and short-story writer. In 1957 he won the Tom-Gallon Award, one of Britain's premier short-story awards.

As a critic he has written for such journals as the *Times Literary Supplement, The Kenyon Review, Spectator,* and *The Listener.* In 1966–67 he was visiting critic and associate editor of *The Kenyon Review;* and in 1968–69 he was a reviewer of fiction for *The Listener.*